Praise for Vicki Lewis Thompson's
Sons of Chance

"*Cowboy Up* is a sexy joy ride, balanced with good-natured humor and Thompson's keen eye for detail. Another sizzling romance from the RT Reviewers' Choice award winner for best Blaze."
—*RT Book Reviews* on *Cowboy Up*

"Vicki Lewis Thompson has compiled a tale of this terrific family, along with their friends and employees, to keep you glued to the page and ending with that warm and loving feeling."
—*Fresh Fiction* on *Cowboys and Angels*

"Intensely romantic and hot enough to singe... her Sons of Chance series never fails to leave me worked up from all the heat, and then sighing with pleasure at the happy endings!"
—*We Read Romance* on *Riding High*

"If I had to use one word to describe *Ambushed!* it would be charming.... Where the story shines and how it is elevated above others is the humor that is woven throughout."
—*Dear Author* on *Ambushed!*

"Top Pick! Thompson continues to do a great job with her popular Sons of Chance series by bringing the entire town of Shoshone and the Last Chance Ranch environment alive in this wonderfully engaging installment."
—*RT Book Reviews* on *Wild at Heart*

Dear Reader,

With a mixture of nostalgia and anticipation I give you the final Sons of Chance book as my Christmas present to the Chance-savvy readers and the newcomers who've just discovered the series. To those who've been with me all the way, we've had a great time, haven't we? To those just joining us, you have some catching up to do!

This moment is nostalgic because I love the Last Chance Ranch. I've mentally lived here for several years, and if the ranch suddenly appeared in 3-D, I'd know exactly where everything is and recognize all the folks. I know many of you feel the same!

But I'm also filled with anticipation, because next summer we'll venture to a cozy ranch outside Sheridan, Wyoming. Don't worry, I won't abandon the Chance brothers! They'll show up occasionally in the new series—Thunder Mountain Brotherhood—debuting in June 2015. You'll also see more of Ben Radcliffe, this book's hero, who lives in Sheridan.

I predict you'll love Thunder Mountain Ranch, which for many years housed foster boys and now needs some help from those guys. But this holiday season, let's focus on the Last Chance! The entire family invites you to a big holiday celebration that includes Sarah's seventieth birthday. You don't want to miss that!

So stay, enjoy and reminisce. Next summer, I invite you to take the half-day drive over to Thunder Mountain Ranch and meet the new gang. In the meantime, let's all raise a glass to a Last Chance Christmas!

Nostalgically yours,
Vicki

Vicki Lewis Thompson

———

A Last Chance Christmas

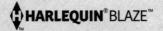

Recycling programs
for this product may
not exist in your area.

ISBN-13: 978-0-373-79827-8

A Last Chance Christmas

Printed in U.S.A.

Vicki Lewis Thompson's passion for travel has taken the *New York Times* bestselling author to Europe, Great Britain, the Greek Isles, Australia and New Zealand. She's visited most of North America and has her eye on South America's rainforests. Africa, India and China beckon. But her first love is her home state of Arizona, with its deserts, mountains, sunsets and—last but not least—cowboys! The wide-open spaces and heroes on horseback influence everything she writes. Connect with her at vickilewisthompson.com, facebook.com/vickilewisthompson and twitter.com/vickilthompson.

Books by Vicki Lewis Thompson

Harlequin Blaze

The Sons of Chance Series

Should've Been a Cowboy

Cowboy Up

Cowboys Like Us

Long Road Home

Lead Me Home

Feels Like Home

I Cross My Heart

Wild at Heart

The Heart Won't Lie

Cowboys & Angels

Riding High

Riding Hard

Riding Home

For more titles by this author, visit the Author Profile page at Harlequin.com.

To the Lone Ranger, my first crush.
A white horse, a deep voice and a mask.
What more could a girl want?

Prologue

Christmas Night, 1990
From the diary of Eleanor Chance

My BROTHER SETH called tonight from Arizona, and we spent a good amount of time bragging about our grandchildren. Seth and Joyce ended up with four kids—three sons and a daughter—while Archie and I only had Jonathan. So it's not surprising that Seth has ten grandchildren to my three.

Not that I'm comparing or complaining. In fact, ten grandchildren on Christmas Day had worn Seth to a frazzle, even though he'd never admit it. I can only imagine.

We had enough ruckus with Jack, Nicky and Gabe trying out their new games. And don't get me started on the subject of NERF footballs. Yes, they're soft and supposedly can be played with in the house, but they inspire all manner of tackling and running and throwing. Archie bought them each one without consulting me.

Seth got a kick out of the NERF football drama.

Then he had to tell me about his three-year-old granddaughter, Molly, who spent the entire day dressed as a princess, complete with tiara. About the only thing I envy Seth is that he has granddaughters as well as grandsons. Molly sounds like a pip, smart and funny. According to Seth, she has her two older brothers buffaloed.

Maybe next spring Archie and I can fly down to spend time with the Gallagher clan. We haven't visited in quite a while. Seth and Joyce came up to Jackson Hole two years ago, but I haven't seen my three nephews and my niece since they were kids. Now they have kids of their own.

According to Seth, everyone's doing great except his daughter Heather. She married a hard-drinking rodeo man, which means they travel a lot. Seth doesn't think they're very happy. They have one son, Cade, who's the same age as little Molly. Seth is worried about what will happen to that tyke as he's tossed from pillar to post.

Makes me thankful that my grandkids are all right here where I can see them every day. I cherish that most of the time. All right, I cherish it all the time, even when they're playing NERF football in the living room. I didn't need that vase anyway.

1

Present Day

AFTER BATTLING ICY roads all the way from Sheridan, Ben Radcliffe was cold and tired by the time he reached Jackson Hole and the Last Chance Ranch. But adrenaline rather than fatigue made him clumsy as he untied the ropes holding a blanket over the saddle he was delivering to Jack Chance.

Jack, the guy who'd commissioned it for his mother Sarah's seventieth birthday, watched the unveiling. The two men stood in a far corner of the ranch's unheated tractor barn in order to maintain secrecy. They'd left their sheepskin jackets on and their breath fogged the air.

This gift would be revealed at a big party the following night, so to keep the secret Ben was masquerading as a prospective horse buyer. It was a flimsy story because buyers seldom arrived in the dead of winter. But the combination of Christmas next week and a major birthday tomorrow had kept Sarah from questioning Ben's arrival.

The entire Chance family, including a few people who weren't technically related to Sarah, had helped pay for this elaborate saddle. Jack's initial reaction was crucial. Ben hoped to God he'd made something worthy of the occasion.

The last knot came loose. Ben's heart rate spiked as he removed the rope and pulled the padding away.

Jack's breath hissed out. "Wow."

"Good?" Ben dared to breathe again.

"Incredible." Jack moved closer and traced the intricate pattern on the leather.

That tooling had taken Ben countless hours, but he thought it showed well against the walnut shade of the leather. Even in the dim light, the saddle seemed to glow. Silver accents he'd polished until his fingers ached were embellished with small bits of hand-picked turquoise from his best supplier. He'd put his heart and soul into this project.

Jack stepped back with a wide smile of approval. "She'll love it."

"That's what I'm hoping." Ben's anxiety gave way to elation. The biggest commission of his life and he'd nailed it—at least, in Jack's opinion, and that counted for a whole lot.

"I have no doubt she will. It *looks* like her—the deep color of the leather, the classy accents, the tooling—she'll go crazy over this. Everyone will." With a smile, Jack turned and held out his hand. "You were the right choice for the job. Thank you."

"You're welcome." Ben shook hands with Jack and returned his smile. "I'll admit I haven't truly relaxed since you came to my shop in October. I wanted to get this right."

"You've obviously worked like a galley slave. I'm not a saddle maker, but I can appreciate the hours that must have gone into this."

"A few."

"Oh, before I forget." Jack took a check out of his wallet. "Here's the balance we owe on it. Now that I've seen the saddle, I'm not convinced you charged enough. That's amazing workmanship."

"It's enough." Ben pocketed the check without looking at it, but knowing it was there and that his bank account was healthy felt really nice. "I love what I do and I feel lucky that it pays the bills, too."

"I predict that soon it'll do more than pay the bills. You have a bright future. Once my brothers get a gander at this, I guarantee they'll both be trying to figure out if a new saddle is in their budgets. I know I'm thinking like that."

Ben laughed. "I'd be happy to cut a deal for repeat customers or multiple orders."

"Oh, yeah. Dangle temptation in my face. Thanks a lot." Jack grinned. "Come on, let's cover this up and get the hell into the house where it's warm. We have a heated shed for your truck, too."

"Sounds good." Ben replaced the blanket and together they moved the saddle stand to the far corner of the tractor barn, farther out of sight.

They passed by a sleigh, which had to be the one Jack had mentioned back in October. Jack had been worried that the carpenter wouldn't finish it before the holidays, but there it was, a one-horse open sleigh worthy of "Jingle Bells." Cute.

Ben gestured to it. "I see your guy came through for you."

"Yeah, thank God. And we've already gone dashing through the snow more times than I can count. Everybody loves it. Hell, so do I. The runners are designed for maneuverability. It can turn on a dime."

Ben laughed as he imagined Jack tearing around the countryside with his new toy. "I'll bet."

"You'll have to take it for a spin while you're here," Jack said as they walked toward the front again. "Oh, and I hope you don't mind the white lie that you're here to look at one of our Paints."

"I don't mind, but speaking of that, which horses did you supposedly show me?"

Jack paused before opening the door. "Let's see. How about Calamity Sam? He's a fine-looking gray-and-white stallion, five years old, could be used as a saddle horse and as a stud."

A gray-and-white Paint. The artistic appeal of a horse with a patterned coat fired his imagination. He'd never made a black saddle, but that might look good with the gray and white. "Any others?"

"You could say I tried to sell you Ink Spot, but you liked Calamity Sam better. Then tell everybody that you have to think about it before you make a final decision."

"And why didn't I bring a horse trailer?"

Jack adjusted the fit of his black Stetson. "That's easy. You saw no point in transporting a horse in this God-awful weather, but you were in the mood to go looking. If you decide on Calamity Sam, you'll pick him up in the spring."

"You'd hold him for me that long?"

Jack's brow creased. "We're making this up to fool my mother. It's not real."

"Yeah, I know, but supposing I actually wanted to look at your horses?"

"Ah." Jack's puzzled expression cleared. "Do you?"

"I might."

"Well, then." Jack stroked his chin and his dark eyes took on a speculative gleam. "In that case, maybe we could work out a little trade, one of our horses for some of your saddle-making skills."

"It's a thought." In the back of his mind, Ben was already designing a black saddle with silver accents. "Right now I don't have a place to keep a horse, but that could change."

"Especially if you take a liking to Calamity Sam."

Ben smiled. "Exactly." The idea of posing as a horse buyer on this trip had sparked his interest in actually buying one. He made saddles for everyone else but didn't have one for himself because he didn't own a horse. Stable horses were okay, but he craved a horse of his own with a custom saddle on its back.

"You're staying for a couple of nights, aren't you?"

"Just overnight. This is your holiday, and I don't want to—"

"Hey, you just brought the coolest gift my mother has ever had, so you can stay as long as you want. We have plenty of room."

"Well, if you're sure."

"Absolutely. The only person staying upstairs is Molly, which leaves three empty bedrooms. Cassidy, our housekeeper, is off visiting family, so you might have to fend for yourself. My brothers and I have our own places, now."

"Who's Molly?"

"My cousin from Arizona. She's here to do genealogy research on the family, but she'll go back to Prescott before Christmas. Don't worry. There's plenty of space if you want to stay on and scope out the horse situation. Unless you have to get back."

"I don't have any plans that can't be changed. So thanks for the hospitality. I might take you up on it." Much depended on whether he felt like an interloper once he met the rest of the family. As usual, he had no holiday gatherings back in Sheridan.

He'd never been part of a big family Christmas, and he was curious about whether it would be the way he imagined. But he was a stranger, so he wouldn't really fit in. On second thought, he shouldn't stay. The horse deal, though, was worth considering.

"You should stay at least three nights," Jack said. "I might not have time to show you the horses tomorrow because we'll be getting organized for Mom's party, but the next day I could."

"How about giving me a preview right now?"

"Now? Aren't you ready for a warm fire and a cold beer?"

"Yeah, but how long would it take to wander through the barn?"

Jack gazed at him. "You're right, and I'd be a damned poor salesman if I didn't take you over there right now, especially if you're considering swapping horseflesh for saddles. My brothers would kill me if I screwed that up." Jack opened the door and ushered Ben out into the cold late afternoon.

Darkness approached, and the two-story log ranch house looked mighty inviting with smoke drifting from the chimney and golden light shining in most of the windows. But the barn looked inviting, too, with its old-fashioned hip-roofed design and antique lamps mounted on either side of the big double doors. Each door had a large wreath on it, decorated with a big red bow.

"Well, look at that," Jack said. "My brother Gabe's over at the barn. That's his truck there. I wonder what he's up to."

"Is he the one who rides in cutting-horse competitions?" After Jack's visit to his shop, Ben had done some research on the Last Chance Ranch. He'd heard of the place, of course, but he'd wanted more in-depth information to guide him in his saddle design.

"He is, and I'm sure he'd love a new saddle. But I warn you he's picky as hell."

"I'd enjoy the challenge." Ben looked forward to meeting the other family members, and if any of them wanted saddles, so much the better. He navigated a narrow path that had been cleared between the tractor barn and the horse barn. Knee-high drifts formed a barrier on either side.

He was used to Sheridan, where snowplows kept the streets passable except during the worst storms. Out here, the Chance family had to use their own resources to deal with weather issues. In the barn where the saddle was hidden, he'd even seen a tractor with a plow attached.

Jack opened the barn door and they were greeted with warmth, light and the satisfying aroma of hay and horses. Ben decided that he wanted a barn. He'd need some kind of shelter if he planned to buy a horse. Some folks left horses outside through the winter, but he'd rather have a barn.

He could build a tack room for his saddle and other

equipment. If he had more than one horse, he'd make a saddle for each of them. Saddles on horses were like boots on a cowboy. If they didn't fit, no amount of padding or stretching would make them feel right. He winced whenever he saw a horse with an ill-fitting saddle. Had to feel damned uncomfortable.

A cowboy with a sandy-colored mustache walked down the wood-floored aisle toward them. "Hey, Jack."

"Hey, Gabe. I'd like you to meet Ben Radcliffe. He just brought Mom one hell of a saddle. You should go see it."

Gabe smiled. "Why do you suppose I'm here?" Then he shook Ben's hand. "Good to meet you, Radcliffe. Thanks for making the trip."

"Glad I could."

Jack unbuttoned his coat. "You snuck over here to get a look at the saddle?"

"I didn't sneak. I drove."

"Yeah, well, you'd better have given your kids a good excuse for doing that, especially Sarah Bianca. If she gets wind that there's a secret present for her grandma hidden somewhere on the ranch, we'll hear about it all day long. Mom will get suspicious and the surprise will be ruined for sure."

"I told them I wanted to check on Persnickety. He's been favoring his right front leg."

Jack frowned. "He has?"

"Well, he *was*. Sort of. But guess what? Now he's all better. Is the saddle in the tractor barn?"

"I thought that was the best place. Go all the way to the back in the right-hand corner. There's a blanket covering it. Take a flashlight."

Gabe pulled his phone out of his jacket pocket. "Get

with the program, bro. Nobody carries a flashlight any-more. We have an app for that."

"I'm sure you do. I'll keep using my Coleman lan-tern, which will still be functioning when your teeny battery is DOA."

Gabe laughed and picked up a battery-operated lan-tern sitting on a shelf. "I just say these things to get your goat, big brother. Works every time."

"Bite me."

"Nah, I've outgrown that. Say, have you done your homework for Molly yet?"

Jack groaned. "Hell, no. Have you?"

"Some of it. The form she gave us is longer than a dead snake. I got bored and quit." Gabe looked over at Ben. "Our cousin from Arizona. She's a history pro-fessor by day but a genealogist by night." He turned to Jack. "Which reminds me. Have you told her about the saddle? Morgan wanted me to ask if Molly's in on the secret."

"I haven't told her. I had to get to know her first and find out if she could be trusted to keep quiet. Now I know she's trustworthy, but there hasn't been a good time to say anything when Mom wasn't around."

"Yeah, and that'd be one more person who could slip up accidentally. Morgan seems to think we should tell her, but I say if it's gone this long, might as well not take the risk." He glanced at Ben. "That means as far as Molly's concerned, you're a prospective horse buyer."

"Got it."

"You might not see much of her, anyway," Jack said. "She spends a lot of time on the computer with her genealogy program. Once she has the family tree all completed, she's going to put it into some kind of book for all of us."

"Sounds nice." It also sounded like something done out of love for family. Ben doubted his family would ever create something similar.

Jack sighed. "I suppose it will be, but all the paperwork is a pain in the ass. I tried to get Josie to do it for me. She filled in her part, but she flatly refused to fill in mine."

"Yeah, Morgan wouldn't do mine, either." Gabe glanced over Jack's shoulder as the barn door opened. "Well, if it isn't Nicky. Whatcha doing here, Nick, old boy?"

"Oh, just happened to have a little spare time." Nick walked toward them.

Jack shoved back his hat. "I don't suppose you're here to check out the saddle or anything like that."

"Maybe." Nick smiled and shook hands with Ben. "You must be Radcliffe. I had a look at your website. Impressive work."

"Thanks." Ben's eye for detail took in the similarities among the brothers—same height and build, same mannerisms. But there were marked differences, too.

Jack's dark hair and eyes suggested he had some Native American blood, while Nick and Gabe showed no evidence of that. Gabe was the fairer of the two. He'd probably been a towhead once. Nick's green eyes made him look as if he belonged in Ireland. Interesting.

"Ben outdid himself on the saddle for Mom," Jack said. "But I hope she doesn't happen to glance out the window when you two yahoos head down to the tractor barn together."

"What about Ben's truck?" Gabe smoothed his mustache. "It's parked right in front of the tractor barn, but he's supposed to be here to see horses, not tractors."

"You can't see the front of that barn from the house." Jack crossed his arms. "But she could see you leave here and walk in that direction."

Nick looked over at Gabe. "Did you say the tractor hitched to the snowplow has a bad starter?"

"No, I didn't—oh, wait." Gabe smiled. "Come to think of it, you're right. You and I need to go check on that. They're predicting a blizzard in a couple of days and we don't want to be caught without a snowplow."

"Just what I was thinking." Nick turned up the collar of his sheepskin jacket.

Gabe did the same and pulled on leather gloves. "Hey, did you do your homework for Molly?"

"I did. Scanned it and emailed it to her this morning."

"Loser."

Nick laughed. "I take it you haven't?"

"Jack hasn't, either." Gabe looked to Jack for backup.

"Haven't found the time," Jack said.

"Yeah, right." Nick sent them both a knowing grin. "Just do it, okay? She's very into this, even if you two aren't."

Gabe blew out a breath. "Yeah, I know she is. Morgan thinks it's endearing. She also thinks Molly should be told about the saddle. You haven't said anything, have you?"

"Nope. If she knows, she didn't get it from me."

"She doesn't know," Jack said. "And she might want to contribute if we told her about it, but we've dealt with the money situation already. Gabe and I think we should just keep it a secret since we're this close and she wasn't part of it from the beginning."

"Fine with me." Nick glanced at his two brothers. "But you really should fill out those forms for her. It's not so much to ask."

"You're right." Jack grimaced. "Otherwise, she'll bug me until I do."

"Yep, guaranteed she will," Gabe said. "I like her okay, but she sure can be a bossy little thing."

Ben listened to the conversation with amusement. Jack had said he'd be sharing the second floor with Molly, who sounded like a determined woman. This trip was becoming more interesting by the minute.

2

SOMEONE WAS PLAYING "Silent Night" on the harmonica. Nostalgia washed over Molly Gallagher and she paused, fingers resting on the computer keyboard. Her Grandpa Seth had played the harmonica, and the gentle sound, especially at Christmastime, always made her think of him.

Harmonicas and cowboys seemed to go together, and her grandpa had been an old-fashioned cowpoke who'd grown up right here in Jackson Hole. He'd even lived in this house for a little while with his sister, Nelsie, and his brother-in-law, Archie. If Molly believed in ghosts, she might think Grandpa Seth had taken up residence down the hall from her bedroom.

"Silent Night" was followed by "O Little Town of Bethlehem." Talk about atmosphere. Snow drifted down outside her window and the scent of pine filled her room. Yesterday she'd helped Aunt Sarah arrange fresh boughs all over the house. With her bedroom door open, she could hear the logs crackling in the giant fireplace downstairs.

Feeling all warm and cozy, Molly went back to entering data in her Excel file. The harmonica player was likely the guy Jack had mentioned was staying down the hall. His name was Ben something-or-other. He'd come to look at the ranch's registered Paints and would be around for a couple of nights. Molly had offered to help out by making his bed and putting clean towels in his bathroom.

Being alone upstairs with four empty bedrooms had been a little spooky. She was glad to share the space with someone, especially if he chose to serenade her every so often with Christmas carols on the harmonica. Hard to believe she'd be leaving in four days. The time had flown by.

Although she'd love to stay and meet everyone who'd be coming in to spend Christmas Eve and Christmas Day, that would mean she'd miss the big Gallagher family celebration in Prescott. So far, she had a perfect record—twenty-eight consecutive holidays spent at the Double Down Ranch. Her parents ran it now that her grandparents were gone, and it was her favorite place in the world.

"O Little Town of Bethlehem" came to a close with a long, drawn-out note embellished by some vibrato. Ben was pretty good on that thing. Then he switched away from carols to play the theme from *Beauty and the Beast.* She'd loved that movie from the first time she'd seen it as a little girl. Belle was the perfect heroine—pretty, brave and well-read.

Plus she was a brunette, and Molly had been thrilled about that, too. The scholarly Belle had been her role model for years. She'd never heard the theme played on a harmonica before, but it worked. It worked so well that she left her chair and moved into the hall so she could hear it better.

What a lovely sound. He really was talented. She moved a few steps closer and then a few steps more. He played with heart, and she could almost imagine him as the Beast longing for his Beauty to show up. That was plain silly, of course. The way her luck went, he'd be old as the hills, or middle-aged and balding.

His bedroom door was open. As the music continued, she edged closer. Now that her curiosity was aroused, she wanted to find out what the man who created such a heavenly sound looked like. But she decided to wait until he'd finished the song. She liked it way too much to interrupt him, and if she suddenly appeared, he'd probably stop playing.

The last note trailed away, and she walked up to the doorway, prepared with a little speech. "That was…" She forgot what she'd intended to say. Ben something-or-other was drop-dead gorgeous.

Why hadn't she brushed her hair before walking down here? Why hadn't she checked to see if she had anything in her teeth? Why hadn't she taken *two measly seconds* to glance in a mirror and find out if her glasses were smudged?

Thinking of that, she whipped them off and cleared her throat. "I'm Molly Gallagher. I live down the hall." *What?* "I mean, I'm *sleeping* down the hall. That is, my room's…that way." She actually pointed. Good God, now she was giving the beautiful man directions.

His eyes were the color of dark chocolate, and they crinkled at the corners when he smiled. "Good to know."

Heat flooded her face. "I didn't mean that as a…

well, never mind. I don't know why I said it. Mostly I wanted to tell you how much I like your harmonica. Your harmonica *playing*, that is."

"Thanks. I didn't know anybody was up here. You were quiet as a mouse."

"Just nibbling away on my computer." Her laugh sounded much too breathless, but he had *such* broad shoulders, and his dark hair curled gently around his ears in a very sexy way. She liked his chin, too, with its little cleft, and she adored his mouth. A harmonica player would be good with his mouth and his tongue. She'd never thought of that before.

"I promise not to play in the middle of the night."

"I wouldn't care." And didn't that sound like she'd become his adoring fangirl? She licked her dry lips. "Actually, I grew up hearing harmonica music. My grandpa would sometimes play me a lullaby before I went to sleep."

"That's very sweet."

"It was more of a bribe. I always put up a fight about going to bed." She had no idea where these idiotic remarks were coming from, but she couldn't seem to make them stop.

She'd prepared herself for some old geezer, probably because she associated harmonicas with her grandfather. Instead she'd found this amazing man, who couldn't be much older than she was. He sat on the edge of a king-sized bed she'd personally made up earlier today. Her filter must be working a little bit, because at least she hadn't blurted out that piece of information.

"I'll bet you did put up a fight about bedtime."

Amusement flashed in his brown eyes. "I'll bet you were one feisty little girl."

"Jack would probably tell you I still am. I think he and Gabe are a little irritated with me."

"Why is that?"

"Oh, there's something I asked them to do and they're both procrastinating. I'm leaving in four days so I gave them each a little nudge. I don't think they appreciated it."

He seemed to be working hard not to laugh.

"Did Jack mention that to you?"

"Just in passing."

"It's only two pages of information for my gene-alogy research. You'd think I'd asked him to write a book."

"Some people hate filling out forms."

She sighed. "I know. Everybody's not detail oriented like I am. I should probably just sit down with each of them and do it interview style. I'll text them and sug-gest that. I mean, if Jack's complaining to you, a vir-tual stranger, I guess he *really* doesn't want to do it."

"He didn't complain all that much. Don't quote me on this, but I think he plans to finish it soon."

"Then I'll wait and see. He might be insulted if I of-fered to write it down for him, as if he's not capable."

"I've only spent a little time with the guy, but I think you're right."

Discussing this matter with Ben had been a good ice-breaker. He felt like a potential friend now. She was still ogling him a little, but she'd recovered from her first stunned reaction. "Sarah told me you were here to look at horses."

"That's right." Something flickered in his gaze the

way it did when someone wasn't telling the whole truth and nothing but the truth.

She caught it because she'd thought all along that driving around looking at horses in this weather was strange. She couldn't shake the suspicion that he was here for some other reason, but she couldn't imagine what that would be. "Did you see any you might be interested in?"

"I did, as a matter of fact. I really like the looks of Calamity Sam."

"Oh, yeah. Me, too. He's one beautiful stallion. Pricey, though, since he gets pretty good stud fees."

"I know. Jack said maybe we could work something out."

So maybe he really was interested in buying one of the Last Chance horses. He might hope to get a better price by coming when business was slow. But asking any more questions would make her seem nosy—which she was, of course. She'd been nosy all her life.

But sometimes she caught herself doing it and backed off. This was one of those times. "Well, I've bothered you long enough. I should get back to my work. If you need anything like more towels or extra pillows, the linen closet is right down there." She gestured to a door on the far side of the hallway. "The housekeeper's on vacation so we're on our own up here."

"Jack told me. I'm pretty good at looking out for myself."

"Great. That's great. Anyway, thanks for the harmonica concert. Please play any time you feel like it. Brings back fond memories for me."

"I'll remember that. Actually, I was about to head

downstairs. Sarah and Pete invited me to have a drink with them before dinner."

"Oh! Is it happy hour already?" Whenever she became involved in a genealogy project, she lost track of time.

"Almost six."

"Then I'll turn off my computer. Last night Sarah had to come upstairs to get me or I would have worked through the whole evening. I'd have hated that because I love hanging out with her and Pete. I'll see you down there, then." She turned to leave.

"I can wait until you shut off your computer."

Thank God she wasn't facing him, because she wouldn't have wanted him to see her reaction to that comment. For sure, her eyes and mouth had popped wide open exactly the way a cartoon character would look when startled. "Um, sure, that would be great. I'll just be a sec. Meet you at the top of the stairs." And she skedaddled out of there.

As she hurried down the hall, she calculated how much repair work she could get away with. Changing clothes was out, so she was stuck with the blah jeans and her old green turtleneck. If she had time to pop in her contacts, Ben might notice that the sweater nearly matched her eyes, but she didn't so he wouldn't.

The best she could hope for was a quick brush through her hair, a fast polish of her lenses and a glance in the bathroom mirror to make sure she didn't have food in her teeth. Refreshing her makeup would take too long, and besides, he'd already seen her like this. If she showed up with lipstick and blusher, that might telegraph her interest in him.

But, truly, she might as well forget about having

any interest in him. It didn't matter how yummy he looked, or how much she loved his harmonica music, or how talented his mouth might be as a result of playing said harmonica. She was leaving in four days and didn't expect to be back in Wyoming any time soon.

She should forget about Ben, whose last name she still didn't know. It wasn't like she was thirsting for male companionship. For example, there was Dennis, the new guy in the history department. He was cute in a nerdy kind of way, and he'd seemed quite fascinated by her when they'd talked during the faculty Christmas party. He'd promised to call after the holidays.

So, there. She had a potential boyfriend and a potential relationship waiting to be cultivated back home. No need to get starry-eyed over some horse-buying, harmonica-playing cowboy who had his feet firmly planted in Wyoming.

Then she walked out of her room and saw those booted feet braced slightly apart as Ben waited for her at the top of the stairs. Oh, Lordy. She'd never looked at a man and instantly fallen into lust. Well, except for unattainable movie stars.

But it was happening this very minute. He'd been impressive sitting on the bed. Standing upright in all his six-foot-plus glory, he made her forget her own name, let alone the name of that guy in the history department.

Then he smiled at her and her knees actually weakened. She'd thought that was a stupid cliché, but apparently not. When she went back for second semester, she'd get one of her friends in the biology department to explain how a brilliant smile from a handsome man could adversely affect a woman's tendons, ligaments, joints and kneecaps.

She hoped she didn't wobble like a Weeble as she joined him at the top landing. "Thanks for waiting for me."

"No problem. By the way, I never introduced myself. I'm Ben Radcliffe."

"I know. I mean, I knew about the Ben part but I'd forgotten your last name." If she'd known he was a walking female fantasy, she would have paid more attention when Sarah mentioned it.

"Okay, now that we have that out of the way, we can—whoops. Hold still for a minute." He leaned toward her.

Her heart leaped into high gear as he reached a hand toward her hair. She'd been told it was her best feature because it was so many rich shades of brown. Maybe he couldn't resist running his fingers through it. That would be a good start.

Then, after he'd buried his fingers in her hair, he could lean even closer and kiss her. Maybe she should take off her glasses to make that maneuver easier, but he'd told her to hold still. She'd have to move a little, though, because he was almost a foot taller than she was. She'd have to stand on tiptoe for a proper kiss.

As his fingers made contact, she closed her eyes and tried to breathe normally. That sure wasn't working. Finally she gulped in some air so she wouldn't pass out and tumble down the curved staircase.

"There you go."

She opened her eyes to discover a piece of dental floss dangling in front of her face.

"It was in your hair."

"Oh." Her cheeks hot, she grabbed the floss and rubbed it between her palms until it was a tiny ball. Then she shoved it in the pocket of her jeans. "Thanks. That's what I get for rushing." She couldn't make herself look at him.

"You have great hair."

That brought her head up. She gazed into his warm brown eyes and said the first thing that popped into her head. "So do you."

"Thank you." The crinkles reappeared at the corners of his eyes because he was smiling again. "I got teased about it as a kid. I guess I looked too girly."

Not anymore. "What do kids know?"

"Not just kids. My dad, too."

"Oh." That made her heart hurt. "Guess you proved him wrong, huh?"

He shrugged. "Doesn't matter if I did or not. We're not that close, anyway."

"Well, that's…" She stopped herself before saying it was too bad. She knew nothing about him, really, or about his family. For him, distance from his father might be a good thing. "That's the way it happens sometimes." She'd honor his obvious wish to make light of what, for her, would be a devastating situation. She couldn't imagine not being close to either of her parents.

"Yep, sure does. Ready?"

"You tell me. I was prepared to walk downstairs wearing dental floss. Do I pass inspection?"

"Now that you mention it, I don't know if you do or not. Back up and do a slow turn for me."

She followed his instructions, although she didn't kid herself that he had ulterior motives for the request.

There wasn't much to see because she'd always been slender, not curvy. If she'd been taller, instead of only five-four, she could have been a runway model.

But not really. The idea had been an obsession of hers as a preteen, when her egghead status had made her feel uncool. A career as a high-fashion model would have soothed her ego. But she'd abandoned that plan when she'd realized, first, she'd never grow tall enough, and second, she'd only be modeling to improve her social standing, which was a dumb reason to get into any line of work.

So, instead, she'd embraced her brainy side, especially her passion for details, specifically historical details. Teaching history during the day and studying genealogy in her spare time made her incredibly happy. In her chosen profession, being an egghead was a good thing.

She finished her circle and glanced up at him. "Okay?"

"Perfect."

Of course he didn't mean that literally, but she couldn't help the squiggle of happiness that danced through her. When a man who looked like Ben declared that she was perfect, she'd take it with a grain of salt, but she'd take it. "Then let's go down."

"Now I'm not sure if I pass inspection or not."

"Don't worry." She smiled at him. "You're perfect, too." That was the main problem with him, in fact. If she were to design her ideal man, he would look exactly like Ben. She just hoped he wouldn't turn out to be the guy who would haunt her dreams once she left Wyoming.

3

BEN WASN'T SURE what to do about his instant attraction to the impish woman descending the staircase beside him. He tended to go for tall and curvy. Molly was short and on the skinny side. He'd never finished college, which didn't matter for his saddle making, but he'd steered away from dating scholars because he wasn't sure how to talk to them. Molly was a college professor.

And yet she didn't act much like one, or the way he thought a college professor would behave. He didn't have a lot of experience to go on, but he'd had no trouble talking to her. He liked talking to her, in fact. She was so full of energy, so *happy*. He imagined that he could see her glowing, and not just when she blushed because she'd put her foot in her mouth.

That was part of why she charmed him. Apparently he flustered her, which made him want to fluster her more just to see the pink bloom on her cheeks. But that didn't explain the visceral tug he'd felt when she'd walked down the hall toward him, or the surge of desire he'd felt when she made a slow turn, allowing him to view her from all sides.

She hadn't done it in a suggestive way, as if trying to showcase her body. Yet he'd had the almost irresistible urge to get his hands on her. He still had that urge. He had no trouble imagining what she'd feel like beneath him, a small but explosive bundle of heat. He had a hunch she'd drive him crazy.

Maybe he was drawn to her because of the advance billing. He'd been curious to meet the woman who had no problem pestering all three Chance men for what she wanted. After watching his mother's mouse-like behavior for years, he admired any female who stood up for herself. He might never marry, but if he did, it would be to someone who refused to be intimidated by anyone, especially him.

"So, where are you from, Ben?"

Her question brought him back to reality. He'd already pictured them in bed together and she didn't even know where he lived. "Sheridan."

"Really? That's fabulous! Maybe you can help me track down two of my relatives, an aunt and a cousin."

"Maybe. I've lived there for seven years."

"I hope so. It's not a huge place. My aunt's married name was Heather Marlowe. At least, that's what it was last time we heard from her, although that was a long time ago. She was in Sheridan then."

"Doesn't ring a bell."

"My cousin's name is Cade. His dad was a bull rider, Rance Marlowe, although he'd be too old to do that now. From what I've heard, he wasn't a very nice guy. Aunt Heather might have divorced him, but nobody knows because she stopped writing or calling."

"Sorry, but I don't think I've met anybody named Marlowe."

Molly sighed. "It was worth a shot. I've investigated online but I got nowhere. Rance followed the rodeo circuit and was never in one place for long. My aunt trailed after him and brought little Cade along, too. Well, he's not so little anymore. He'd be the same age as I am, twenty-eight."

He considering pointing out that she was still little, even at twenty-eight, but he figured she'd probably had her fill of short-person jokes. "So they might have had some tough times financially along the way?"

She paused at the foot of the stairs and turned to him. "I wouldn't be surprised. Why?"

"They might have made use of social services there. I know a retired social worker. Maybe she'd remember something, or could ask around."

"That's a great idea. I didn't think of that, but it gives me another avenue. Thanks!"

"She lives not too far from Sheridan at a place called Thunder Mountain Ranch. I—" He caught himself right before he screwed up. He'd been about to announce that he'd made a couple of saddles for Rosie and Herb, but his profession wasn't supposed to be common knowledge yet. "The Padgetts are good people. He's a retired equine vet. For years they also took in foster boys, but they don't do that anymore. Anyway, Rosie knows a lot of people in town. She might have information."

The tension eased from her eyes and she smiled. "I'd run out of ideas, so I'm thrilled to have a new lead. My family always wondered what became of Cade, especially my grandpa."

"The harmonica player."

"Yes. Losing touch with Aunt Heather and Cade made him sad. And of course Heather's my dad's sister. I think he's resigned to the idea that she doesn't want to hang around with the Gallagher family anymore, but he's told me that he wonders where she is. When I started working on this family tree project, tracking them down was one of my goals, especially because my dad still thinks about them."

"Then I wish you luck with it. Now that I know what names to listen for, I'll pay more attention once I get back home. Maybe I'll stumble across somebody who's heard of them."

"Excellent! I'll give you my phone number in case you find anything. You'll be my man in Sheridan."

He couldn't help grinning. "Okay."

Her cheeks turned that wonderful shade of pink again. "That didn't come out quite right."

"It came out fine as far as I'm concerned."

Her blush deepened. "Um, well…I didn't mean to imply that I considered you *my*..." Then she groaned. "I'm going to stop now before I make this worse than it already is. Sarah's going to wonder what the heck we're standing here yakking about. Let's go get us some drinks."

"Works for me." Still smiling, he walked beside her into the living room. She was not a flirt by any stretch, and yet she was clearly interested in him. Earlier he'd wondered what to do about his attraction to her. He might not have to do a damned thing except wait and let nature take its course.

The ranch's beautiful setting wouldn't hurt, either. The living room looked like a scene out of a Christmas card, with pine boughs and ribbons everywhere, plus candles on the mantel. Flames danced in the big stone fireplace, and a ten-foot Scotch pine in the corner glittered with lights, ornaments and garlands.

Sarah and Pete both got up from their leather armchairs. Through Ben's cursory internet research, he'd discovered that Sarah's first husband, Jonathan, had died several years ago and she'd since married Pete Beckett. Pete was tall, like Sarah, and lanky, with gray hair and gentle blue eyes. He was a philanthropist who'd dreamed up the Last Chance's summer program for disadvantaged kids. He had the relaxed air of someone who'd found his place in the world. Ben wondered if that time would ever come for him.

Sarah put down her wineglass. "I thought I heard you two out in the hall."

As Sarah made the introductions, Ben stepped forward and shook hands with Pete, who'd been one of the biggest contributors to the saddle fund. "It's a pleasure."

Obviously Pete wasn't about to give anything away at the zero hour. "I admire your can-do spirit." He raised his glass in Ben's direction. "I'm not sure I'd drive all the way from Sheridan to look at horses in this weather."

"I'm used to the weather and I had some free time. Jack promised I wouldn't be in the way." Ben had been prepared to like the guy, and Pete's casual friendliness didn't disappoint him.

"Heck, no," Pete said. "Always room for one more at a party. Right, Sarah?"

"Absolutely. The more the merrier. It isn't every day a girl turns seventy."

Pete gasped and placed a hand over his heart. "You're that old?"

"Stuff a sock in it, Peter." Sarah laughed. "I'm still younger than you. Now, please get Ben something to drink while I pour Molly a glass of wine. I already know that's what she wants."

"Yes, I sure do. That's a terrific red wine. I'm stocking up on some when I get home."

Pete turned to Ben. "What can I get for you?"

"Jack and I each had a bottle of dark beer this afternoon. Can't remember the brand. I wouldn't mind another one of those if you have it."

Pete set his glass on a coaster. "Let's mosey down to the kitchen and find out if there's a cold one in the fridge. If Jack likes it, we probably have a supply." Once they were in the hallway and out of earshot, Pete lowered his voice. "I had a chance to talk to Jack and he raved about the saddle."

"Good. I'm glad he's happy."

"I want to see it, but I haven't come up with a good excuse to go out to the tractor barn without making Sarah suspicious."

"Nick and Gabe have looked at it, and they seem satisfied."

"Damn. My curiosity is killing me. I wish everybody who chipped in could be here tomorrow for the big reveal, but several couldn't come for both her birthday *and* Christmas. So they asked her when she'd rather have them arrive, and she picked Christmas."

"So, who won't be coming tomorrow?"

"Jack's two half-brothers, Wyatt and Rafe Locke and their wives will wait and come for Christmas. I'm pretty sure their mother Diana also will be here then.

She's Jack's mother, too, of course, but it's hard for me to think of her that way."

"Hang on. Sarah isn't Jack's biological mother?"

"No. She adopted him after she married Jonathan. I don't blame Jack for procrastinating on that family tree project of Molly's. His part is complicated. His biological mother, Diana, divorced his dad when Jack was a toddler. She left Jack here, ran off to San Francisco and married this guy Locke. They had twin boys, Rafe and Wyatt."

"That must have been tough on Jack."

"Yeah. Having his mom leave was bad enough, but he didn't know she'd had two more kids until Wyatt showed up here one day, a couple of years ago." Pete led Ben through the large dining room and into the kitchen, Mary Lou Sims's domain.

Ben had met her earlier when he and Jack had come into the kitchen looking for beer.

Mary Lou closed a door on the double oven and turned, her fly-away gray hair curling in the moist heat. "Hi, guys. Let me guess. Ben wants another beer like the one he had before."

"That's right," Pete said. "We got any more?"

"You know we do." Mary Lou crossed to the commercial-sized refrigerator. "Jack sees to it." She took out a bottle. "Want a glass, Ben?"

"No, thanks. The bottle's fine."

Mary Lou twisted off the cap and smiled as she handed the bottle to him. "I've been hearing great things about that saddle. Everybody says it's gorgeous."

Pete rolled his eyes. "And everybody needs to quit talking about it. Sure as the world, Sarah's going to overhear one of those conversations and figure out what's up."

"Aw, we're all being careful." Mary Lou waved a dismissive hand. "We have less than twenty-four hours until the unveiling. It'll be fine."

"I hope you're right. How soon before dinner's ready?"

"Give me another thirty minutes or so."

"Will do. Thanks, Mary Lou." Pete put an arm around her for a quick hug. "You're the best."

She laughed. "Yes, I am, and don't ever forget it."

"I wouldn't dare. Sarah would kick me out. Come on, Ben. Let's go join the women."

Ben had been sorting through what Pete had told him about Jack and his biological mother. "Is Diana Native American?"

"Half-Shoshone, half-Caucasian, which is where Jack gets his coloring."

Ben nodded. "I wondered about that. So, Jack has two half-brothers on his mother's side, Wyatt and Rafe, and two on his dad's side, Nick and Gabe. That's wild. How does Sarah feel about Diana coming around?"

Pete smiled. "I think the first time was awkward, but she's…amazing. She's forgiven Diana, even though the woman left her kid and never looked back."

"Wow."

"That's not all. Diana also kept his existence and her former marriage a secret from her new family for years. But when Sarah realized how miserable Diana was about it all, she accepted her as part of the family. I don't know if Sarah's forgiven Nick's mother, though."

"You mean Sarah isn't Nick's mother, either?"

"Nope. After Diana left Jonathan, he went sort of

crazy and had an affair with a free spirit who was just passing through. She kept her pregnancy to herself and had Nick without notifying Jonathan. When Nick was six months old, his mother died in a sky-diving accident. Baby Nick arrived in a cab with a lawyer, and Sarah took the little guy in and raised him as her own. But she doesn't have kind words for Nick's mother."

"I'll bet not. Sounds like one flakey lady."

"One who paid the price for it." As they neared the end of the hallway, Pete lowered his voice again. "Regarding the saddle, I figure we'll just leave it on display in the living room until Christmas. I doubt the weather will be good enough for her to try it out, anyway, and everyone can see it when they walk in."

"Sounds good. Oh, and don't be surprised if I end up buying a horse. I asked Jack to show me some prospects this afternoon."

Pete laughed. "You did? That's terrific. Everything's working out great, isn't it?"

"Looks like it." They entered the living room and he noticed Sarah sitting alone, sipping her wine and gazing into the crackling fire. "Where's Molly?" He hadn't realized how much he'd anticipated seeing her until she wasn't there.

"She told me your suggestion about her cousin Cade, and I thought she should call right now. After dinner might be too late, and tomorrow it'll be a zoo around here. She could get sidetracked and forget. So she went to look up the place online to see if she could get the number."

"That's great." Ben hadn't expected Molly to act on his suggestion this fast. He had the number saved in his phone, but no doubt she'd found it online by now.

Which meant she was already calling. If she mentioned that she'd heard about them from him, they could easily tell her that he'd made a couple of saddles for them. That, in itself, wouldn't be bad unless she came down and asked about his saddle-making business in front of Sarah.

If Sarah learned what he did for a living, she'd probably put it all together. His only hope was that if Molly got the information from the Padgetts, she'd figure out the secret and keep it to herself.

Pete sat in the chair next to Sarah's. That left one empty chair and the sofa. Ben noticed Molly's wine glass on the coffee table in front of the sofa, so he sat there, too, hoping to be next to her. Close proximity would give him more options if he had to suddenly keep her from saying something incriminating.

"What's this about Molly's cousin?" Pete picked up his drink.

Sarah combed her silvery hair back with one hand. "She wants to pick up his trail in Sheridan, which was the last address they had for him and his mother. It's a happy coincidence that Ben is from there. You're sure you don't know anybody named Marlowe, Ben?"

"I'm still thinking, and I'll keep my ears open once I get back, but the name doesn't sound familiar."

"I haven't paid much attention to rodeo stars over the years," Sarah said. "So I wouldn't recognize the name Rance Marlowe even if he had been well-known."

Pete shook his head. "Me, either. Did Molly ask the boys?"

Ben got a kick out of Pete's reference to three grown men as *boys*, but the Chance brothers would probably always be *the boys* to Sarah and Pete.

"I'm sure she asked them." Sarah chuckled. "That girl is like a quiz-show host when it comes to questions. She has a million of them. And she loves to dig into what she calls *archives*. I let her look through Jonathan's old trunk full of papers and souvenirs, which she adored, and then I let her read my mother-in-law's diaries covering all the years she and Archie lived here. You'd have thought I'd offered Molly a sack of gold."

"She's fun to have around," Pete said. "I'm going to miss her when she leaves on Monday. But getting back home for Christmas is important to her. She's really big on family."

"I gathered that," Ben said.

"Well, so am I." Sarah took another sip of her wine. "I'll admit when I married Jonathan I didn't realize how important the whole concept of family would become to me. I'm an only child, so my original family consisted of three people. Now I find myself surrounded with an entire clan and it's wonderful."

"And I'm lucky enough to be part of that clan," Pete said. "I'm so thankful that Sarah agreed to let me into the club."

Ben felt as if he'd stumbled into a foreign land where he could barely speak the language. He'd heard people talk about the importance of family, but he'd never understood it on a gut level. His experience growing up had taught him the destructive nature of family ties.

Sarah glanced over at him. "Speaking of that, do you have any siblings, Ben?"

"An older brother in Colorado." He never knew what to say when such questions came up, or how to answer them so the questions would stop. But in this case, with all the talk about bonding, he might have a way out. "We're not close."

Sympathy flashed in Sarah's blue eyes. "I'm sorry."

Ben shrugged and used Molly's earlier response, one he'd thought was brilliant at the time. He'd keep it in mind for any future conversations regarding his family. "That's the way it happens sometimes."

"I know it does, but…" Sarah hesitated. "I hope being in the middle of this crazy group doesn't bother you."

"Not at all." This much he could say with conviction. "I like it."

4

MOLLY KEYED IN the number for Thunder Mountain Ranch with some misgivings. Despite what she'd told Ben, she was conflicted about what she might uncover with this phone call. If Rosie Padgett had no knowledge of Heather or Cade, then Molly was back where she started.

But if the woman had heard of them, that meant they'd contacted social services and very likely had struggled to make a life for themselves. Molly didn't remember her Aunt Heather much at all, but her dad sure did. Heather was his sister, after all, and the news might not be very good.

A woman answered the phone. "Thunder Mountain Ranch."

Well, she'd come this far. Molly took a deep breath. "Hi. I'm Molly Gallagher, and I'm looking for information on my cousin, Cade Marlowe, or his mother, Heather. A friend suggested I call and see if you knew anything about them."

"Cade Marlowe?"

"Yes. His father's a bull rider named Rance, but I'm

sure he's retired from that by now. The last letter my family got from Heather was postmarked in Sheridan, but that was years ago. I'm trying to find out if anybody remembers them or has a forwarding address."

"I'm sorry, but I don't know anybody named Cade Marlowe."

"Oh." In spite of her desire for information, she was relieved.

"But if you want to leave your number, I could ask around. Someone might have heard something."

"Thank you. You must be Mrs. Padgett. The friend who suggested I call is Ben Radcliffe."

"Oh, Ben!" The woman's voice warmed. "Yes, I'm Rosie Padgett. Ben's such a great guy, and when it comes to making saddles, he's a real artist."

"Um, yes, he certainly is." *Ben was a saddle maker?*

As she gave her number to Rosie Padgett and said her goodbyes, she kept thinking about Ben's profession. His odd timing for coming to look at horses coincided with Sarah's birthday—a significant one, at that. She'd wondered all along why Jack would agree to host a potential customer during his mother's big celebration. Jack didn't strike her as the kind of man who put business ahead of family gatherings.

Ben could have come after Christmas, or he could have waited until the weather warmed. Yet here he was, staying in the bosom of the family and attending Sarah's birthday party. But if he'd designed a custom saddle for Sarah, then his sudden appearance the day before her birthday made perfect sense. And of course he'd be invited to stay so he could see her reaction to it.

After booting up her computer, Molly searched for Ben's saddle-making operation. Once she found the site and scrolled through the photos of his work, she was almost positive this was why he was here. And it was supposed to be a surprise.

Well, cool. She'd always loved uncovering secrets. Knowing that Ben was an artisan on a secret mission made him more intriguing than ever. She wasn't the least bit artistic, but she admired those who were.

She knew Ben was good with his mouth because he played a damned fine harmonica. If he'd landed a commission from the Chance family to create a saddle for their beloved matriarch, then he must be good with his hands, too. Add in his fine physique, and it amounted to the sort of man very few women could resist.

She wondered where the saddle was hidden. Probably not in the house where Sarah might accidentally find it. He wouldn't have left it in his truck where it would be difficult for her cousins to see it. The barn wasn't a good spot, either, because Sarah might go down there. She loved taking bits of carrot to Bertha Mae, her favorite horse.

"Molly?" Sarah's voice traveled up the stairs. "Are you having any luck? Dinner's ready."

"I'll be right down!" She shut off her computer.

Then, because she could, she brushed her hair again and put a touch of blusher on her cheeks and the merest hint of gloss on her lips. She'd lived with two brothers, so she knew that most men didn't notice subtle makeup. They just thought a woman looked good and assumed it was her own healthy color coming through.

When she reached the bottom of the stairs, Sarah was there holding a wine glass. "I thought you'd want to take the rest of your wine in to dinner."

"Great! Thank you." She followed Sarah over to the hallway where Pete and Ben waited for them.

"What happened with the Padgetts?" Ben asked. "Did you talk to them?"

"I talked to Rosie Padgett. Very nice lady. She didn't know anybody named Cade Marlowe, but she took my name and number in case she can find out anything through her contacts with social services." She couldn't spend much time looking at Ben because she was liable to start smiling. She knew his secret, and it might show.

"Well, that's something, anyway." Ben sounded wary. He might be worried she'd spill the beans. "You never can tell. She might turn up some information that would help you."

Molly wished she could reassure him that she wouldn't reveal the secret. "She might, although I realized when I made the call that I had mixed feelings. What if she finds out something bad happened to my aunt or my cousin, or both of them? I've always assumed I'd find them and orchestrate a touching reunion with the rest of the family."

"That's because you're an optimist," Pete said. "Don't ever apologize for that. It's an admirable trait."

"Yes, but given the fact that we've heard nothing from either of them in years, what are the odds that they're both okay?" She saw the hesitation in each of their expressions. "See, maybe I don't want to keep searching. Maybe I don't want to know the truth."

Sarah put an arm around her shoulders. "You could call that lady back in the next few days and tell her you've changed your mind. It's nearly Christmas. I doubt she'll start investigating until the New Year."

"Thanks. I might do that. Hey, aren't we supposed

to head to the dining room? As I recall, Mary Lou doesn't take kindly to people who are late for dinner."

"She doesn't," Pete said. "And she told me to give her thirty minutes or so. It's been forty. I think we'd better move it." He started off with Sarah at his side.

Ben followed, but Molly put a restraining hand on his arm. When he turned to her, she mouthed the words *I know.*

His eyes widened.

"I won't say anything," she murmured before starting down the hall.

"Thanks." Ben matched her stride and kept his voice low. "I was worried."

"Don't be."

He let out a breath. "I'm so glad you have a brain."

That made her laugh. "Me, too."

They continued down the hall to the small family dining room adjacent to the larger one used when the hands gathered for lunch every day. Molly loved that meal, too, because the atmosphere was completely different. The main dining room had four round tables that each seated eight, and many days they were all filled.

The Chance brothers attended whenever possible, sometimes with their wives. Gabe's wife, Morgan, often brought all three of their kids when she came, and Jack's wife, Josie, would bring little Archie so he could play with his cousins. Nick's vet practice sometimes kept him away, but his wife, Dominique, liked to be there if she wasn't in the middle of mounting one of her photography shows. When their adopted son Lester wasn't in school, he came to lunch, too. Add in the ranch hands, and the room became a noisy free-for-all.

Tonight, though, the room was in shadows and light

beckoned from the more intimate family dining room through a set of double doors. A rustic metal chandelier hung over a linen-covered table set with china, crystal and silverware. Molly felt the family connection here, because gracious living had been a part of her heritage, too.

She'd researched her great-grandfather and great-grandmother Gallagher, parents of her Grandpa Seth and her Great Aunt Nelsie. The Gallaghers, it turned out, had traveled from Baltimore and had brought with them the customs of a genteel society. So when she sat at this table at the Last Chance Ranch and unfolded her cloth napkin, she thought about how the tradition of elegant dining had been passed down through three generations.

Hers was the fourth, and she already used cloth napkins in her small rental home. She was collecting silver and china. After she had her own family, she'd pull out all the stops.

Sarah and Pete sat across the table from Molly and Ben. While Mary Lou served the dinner, Ben asked questions about the breeding program at the Last Chance. He mentioned his interest in Calamity Sam and suggested he might begin a breeding program of his own in Sheridan. If Molly hadn't known his actual mission had been to bring Sarah's birthday gift, she'd swear he'd come for the reason he'd given.

Pete and Sarah discussed the horses with great enthusiasm. Molly was out of her depth when it came to horse breeding, so she spent a lot of time listening and watching. Mostly she paid attention to the interaction between Ben and Pete as they kept up the fiction that Ben was here as a buyer.

They were both playing their cards very close to the vest. Once or twice she caught a look that passed between them, but if Sarah noticed anything, she didn't say so. Smart lady.

Sarah must have questioned Ben's presence here the night before her birthday celebration. She might suspect he had brought some big surprise with him. But, if so, she'd probably decided not to ask any questions and risk spoiling whatever surprise her husband and sons had cooked up for her.

Now Molly was part of the charade, too, and she loved that. When Ben glanced over at her and gave her a wink, her toes curled. Nothing like a shared secret to bring two people closer together.

She enjoyed their current proximity, in fact. Having him seated within touching distance was quite arousing. His aftershave tantalized her and she found herself listening for the pattern of his breathing and imagining she could feel his body heat.

But she had to find out if the attraction between them was mutual. That meant spending some time alone with him. A bolder woman might walk right down to his bedroom tonight, but that wasn't her style. She had something more subtle in mind.

They all lingered over dessert as the conversation turned to the party, which would begin at four the following day. Mary Lou came out with more coffee and stayed long enough to confirm tomorrow's itinerary.

Sarah glanced at her. "I'll be up by seven to help you bake cookies. Morgan and Josie will be over around ten with the kids."

"Got it." Mary Lou gathered up the dessert plates. "I'm off to bed so I'll be rested up for that crew."

Sarah grinned. "It'll be fun."

"It's always fun, but it's also exhausting. 'Night, all."

Molly had been so focused on Ben that she'd forgotten tomorrow morning Sarah and Mary Lou were going to let the grandkids decorate Christmas cookies. After Mary Lou left, she turned to Sarah. "Will I be in the way if I come down to help?"

"Absolutely not! I was hoping you would. The more adults to help manage the frosting and sprinkles, the better."

"Then I'll set my alarm and be down by seven, too."

"Great." Sarah picked up her coffee cup. "Those kids always look forward to it, and then they'll get to show off their work at the party." She looked over at Ben. "I'm afraid it'll be a little wild around here tomorrow. You might want to grab a book and hide out in the barn."

"Actually, I'd like to help. I'm no good at decorating cookies, but if you need furniture rearranged, I can do that."

"Then you're hired." Sarah smiled at him. "We have to move all the furniture against the walls to create space for dancing. With all the people coming, it'll be crowded out there."

"We'll manage," Pete said. "It wouldn't be a Chance party if we didn't dance."

"But we might have to do it in shifts." Sarah laughed. "Molly, you could make up an Excel sheet and assign us all time slots."

"I could, but I think Jack would tear it up. He's not the type to be assigned a time slot."

Pete smiled. "No, he's not. We'll work it out. So we bump into each other. So what? We're family."

"I don't have to dance," Ben said. "I'm a guest, not family."

"Nonsense." Sarah frowned at him. "As our guest you most certainly should dance. But I guess I should ask if you even like to."

"I do."

"Then you'd better join in," Pete said. "Jack is big on getting everybody out on the floor for at least a few numbers. He's currently teaching all the kids. I guess you could say he's the Last Chance's dance master. If I hadn't been able to two-step, I'm not sure he would have let me marry Sarah."

"And we'll have live music, Ben. A couple of our ranch hands play guitar." Sarah brightened as if inspiration had just hit. "Did I hear you playing a harmonica earlier tonight?"

"Yes, ma'am."

"I'll bet Trey and Watkins would love to have you add your harmonica to the mix, if you're willing."

"Uh, well…sure." Ben looked pleased. "I'd like that. Sounds like fun."

Sarah clasped her hands together. "I do love parties!" Then she beamed at Molly. "I'm so glad you could be here for this one. I wish we could magically transport your whole family up here, too."

"Me, too, but then you'd have to knock out a couple of walls."

"True. Your family's even bigger than ours. I'm losing track of who's who in the Gallagher clan. I remember you and your brothers very well, but I can't tell you the names of their wives and kids without looking it up."

"I know, and I'll be better about sending emails and

pictures from now on. I'm the one the family has put in charge of doing that. What a shocker."

Sarah took another drink of her coffee. "I don't know that we have anybody in that role. We should, though. Now that we can connect online, we should all be better informed about each other."

"We can work on that, but I hope you and Pete are serious about flying down next spring. My folks would love it."

"Oh, we are," Pete said. "I haven't been to Arizona in years. I'm stoked about going."

Sarah took a deep breath and pushed back her chair. "And I'm ready for bed. We have a big day tomorrow. The rest of you can stay here as long as you like, but I'm thinking Mary Lou has the right idea. Time to turn in."

"Yeah, it is for me, too." Pete stood. "But you kids are welcome to hang out here for awhile. Mary Lou won't mind if you help yourself to more coffee and dessert if you clean up after yourselves."

"I'll just finish what I have in my cup," Ben said. "It's great stuff. Then I'll be off to bed, too. It's been a long day."

"I'm sure, driving on those icy roads." Pete tucked an arm around Sarah's waist. "See you both in the morning."

Sarah said good-night, too, and then Molly had her wish, to spend some time alone with Ben. Once Pete and Sarah were out of earshot, she spoke, but kept her voice down. "Rosie Padgett said you were an artist with saddles, and then I knew what you were really here for."

Ben turned sideways in his chair and gazed at her.

"That was nice of her to say, but I sure as hell didn't think it through when I suggested you should call them. I guess it never occurred to me that you'd call now, before the birthday party."

She mirrored his position so she could look at him as they talked. "I probably wouldn't have if Sarah hadn't encouraged me. As you could probably tell, I wasn't sure I wanted to hear what Rosie Padgett had to say."

"I know, and I didn't think about the fact that if your cousin had ended up at Thunder Mountain, then your aunt…well, I can't see that being a good thing where she was concerned."

"No. But he wasn't there, so that leaves the mystery unsolved. I wonder if I should leave it alone and imagine they're doing well but have no interest in reconnecting with their family."

"That could be the truth. You might not have been aware of problems between your aunt and your grandparents, but that doesn't mean there weren't any."

She thought about that for a moment and finally shook her head. "I get what you're saying, and I suppose anything's possible, but Grandpa Seth and Grandma Joyce were kind, gentle people. According to my dad, Aunt Heather was a happy person until she hooked up with Rance Marlowe. Then she got pregnant with Cade and…well, there's never been a divorce in my family."

"Wow, that's unusual."

"I know, and most people who hear that assume it's because problems were swept under the rug. I think it's because they were brought out in the open and dealt with. Heather was the big exception. When she had problems with Rance, she cut off communication and hid their troubles from everybody."

"And you're worried about how that turned out."

"Yes. I thought we'd all be better off knowing the truth, but now I'm not so sure."

Ben sighed. "Well, I don't have any advice. My knowledge of family dynamics is sadly lacking."

"Why?"

He met her gaze and smiled. "I should have known you'd ask that. Which means I shouldn't have made the remark in the first place. Sorry. I'd rather not get into it right now."

Although his tone was friendly and he was doing his best to be polite, she felt a brick wall go up. She couldn't blame him. They'd met a few hours ago. Just because she'd blabbed some of her family information didn't mean that he'd want to do the same. "That's fine. Let's switch topics."

He polished off the last of his coffee. "To what?"

"The saddle you brought here. Where is it?"

He laughed. "You know, I've only been around you for a little while, but somehow I knew you'd ask that question. Now that you know about the saddle, its whereabouts is driving you nuts, isn't it?"

"Yes."

"I guess I can trust you."

"You can. I wouldn't ruin this surprise for anything."

"It's in the far back corner of the tractor barn under a blanket."

"Who's seen it?"

"Jack, Gabe and Nick. That's it."

She gave him her most winsome smile, the one even her brothers had never been able to resist. "Please take me out there. I want to see it, too."

5

BEN SHOULD HAVE seen this coming. Molly was the most inquisitive woman he'd ever run across, and now that she'd learned about the secret present for Sarah, of course she'd want to see it. She'd want to be one of the privileged few who knew what was coming when the saddle was presented tomorrow evening.

And the fact of the matter was, he wanted to show it to her. He was proud of that saddle and after all three Chance brothers had given it a thumbs-up, he felt pretty confident that Molly would like it, too. Still, he needed to think of the logistics.

He considered what they'd have to go through. "It's damned cold out there. I'm sure the temperature's dropped considerably since I was out, and it was freezing, then."

"I know. We'll bundle up and go fast."

"It's snowing."

"Not very hard. A few flakes. The shoveled paths should still be fine if we go right away. Please?"

That smile of hers was something. It made her eyes light up and put a cute little dimple in her left cheek.

He felt like kissing her, but her glasses would be in the way so he didn't act on the impulse. Besides, she'd asked him to take her out to see his saddle, not kiss her.

"Come on, Ben. It'll be fun." She pushed back her chair and picked up her coffee cup and saucer. "We'll just put these in the dishwasher, pull on our duds, and be off."

He stood and collected his dishes. "I'll bet you got your brothers in all kinds of trouble when you were a kid."

"Yes, but they never regretted it. I had great ideas. Even if we were punished…well, mostly they were punished because they got blamed…they still had fun."

Ben laughed. "I'd love to hear their side of that someday."

"You should! You totally should come to Prescott for a visit. It's a cute little town. You'd like it."

"We'll see." Whoops. He wasn't sure how it had happened, but suddenly she was inviting him to Prescott so he could meet her brothers.

He wondered how they'd react to a guy who had no intention of starting a family, ever. That wouldn't work for Miss Molly. Her brothers would probably escort him right out the door. If they thought for one minute he'd misled their baby sister, he might be run out of town on a rail.

But that was a moot point, because he wouldn't be going to Prescott. If he had any sense, he wouldn't have told her where the saddle was, but she had a way of making him say things he shouldn't. Now he had to take her there, because if he didn't, she'd go by herself. He wasn't about to let her do that.

They climbed the stairs together and separated at

the top to go to their respective rooms and suit up. He wound a wool scarf around his neck before pulling on his sheepskin coat. He left it open so he wouldn't roast, made sure his fleece-lined leather gloves were in the pockets and settled his Stetson on his head.

What he needed was a lined hat with earflaps, but he hadn't brought one on this trip. He hadn't expected to be going outside in subzero weather. But then, he hadn't counted on a little bit of a thing winding him around her pinky finger, either. At the last minute, he pocketed his phone so he could use its flashlight feature. Jack might not think much of that convenience, but Ben used his all the time.

As he walked out of his room, Molly appeared wearing a puffy, bright-red jacket, a red knit hair band that covered her ears, a red knit cap and rubber boots. She looked adorable.

They met at the top of the stairs once again, and he realized she held mittens in her hand, not gloves. Who wore mittens anymore? She did, apparently.

She waved them at him. "A gift from one of my sisters-in-law," she said in a low voice. "She's just learning to knit. This is their first and maybe their only outing, but I wanted to tell her I used them in Wyoming and this trip to the tractor barn won't require me to do anything complicated with my fingers."

Her low-pitched comment, probably designed to keep from waking the household, shouldn't make him think of sex, but it did. He pictured the interesting things she could do with her fingers if they were free to roam over his naked body. Presently they were about as far from naked as they could get without being zipped into a hazmat suit.

Something was different about her, other than all the stuff she'd put on to guard against the cold, but at first he couldn't figure out what it was. Then he did. He kept his voice down, too. "Where are your glasses?"

"I popped in my contacts. My glasses would just fog up the minute I stepped outside and started breathing."

"So why don't you wear contacts all the time? Do they bother you?"

"Not really. I just…like my glasses. I know that sounds silly, but I started wearing them when I was a kid, and they're *me* in a way that contacts aren't. It's a cliché, but I feel smarter with them on. Now, see, you're smiling because you think that's ridiculous."

"No, I'm smiling because I like you."

"You do? How do you mean that, exactly?"

He laughed softly. "I keep forgetting that you have to analyze everything."

"That's true, but I just realized I'm getting very hot in this coat, so forget about that question for now. We can talk about it after we come back from the tractor barn and take off all these clothes."

"Depending on how much you plan to take off, we should definitely talk about it."

She blushed. "I didn't mean it like *that*."

"Too bad." Chuckling, he started down the stairs. She was the wrong woman for him. The absolute worst choice he could make. But when she stood there looking so cute and talking about taking off her clothes, he couldn't seem to remember that.

He paused in front of the door to button his coat and put on his gloves. Then he turned up his collar.

She pulled a knitted red scarf out of her pocket. "My sister-in-law knitted this before she tackled the mittens." Molly wrapped it around her neck and then around her nose and mouth so only her eyes showed.

When that was all he could see, he became aware of what a beautiful green they were, and how her long lashes framed them. She might love her glasses, and in a way he preferred that look on her, too. But without her glasses, he could more easily picture her stretched out in his bed, gazing up at him. He'd be wise not to dwell on that or he'd really overheat standing in the entryway.

Last, she put on her mittens, which were too big. "Don't fit very well." Her voice was muffled by the scarf as she moved her hands and the mittens turned into flippers.

He bit the inside of his cheek so he wouldn't laugh. Then, moving cautiously, he opened the front door.

She gasped as frigid air engulfed them.

"We don't have to go."

She shook her head and stepped out onto the porch.

He followed her out, closed the door and took the action any man in this situation would. He wrapped his arm around her shoulders and held her close as they navigated down the steps. Close was a relative term in this case. Holding on to her was like holding onto a blow-up Christmas yard decoration. He kept losing his grip because she was so squashy and slippery.

It might have been the coldest walk he'd ever taken in his life. Without any pavement or large buildings giving off heat, the air bit through his coat as if he'd walked out bare-chested. His nipples tightened in response to the icy temperature until they actually hurt.

But she'd been right about the snowfall. The flakes were lazy and slow. That could change at any time, though, so he planned to make this a very quick trip.

The shoveled path led to the horse barn, then branched off to the tractor barn. It was narrow, but by hugging her against him, he was able to steer them along it without either of them stepping into the crusted drifts on each side.

The horse barn was heated, as he'd discovered this afternoon. He considered making a stop there to warm up and decided she wouldn't go for that. She didn't strike him as a woman who took very many detours in life.

Besides, the sooner they got to the tractor barn and looked at the saddle, the sooner they could get back to the cozy ranch house. He thought he'd become used to Wyoming winters, but he'd never been outside in a landscape like this, where security lights and a pale moon reflected off untrampled snow. Beyond the soft glow coming from the house and the barn, the surroundings were completely dark.

No sound greeted him, either, not even the hoot of an owl. He knew this was wolf country, but they were silent, too. The frozen world was completely still, without even a breeze. For that he was grateful. They didn't need a wind-chill factor right now.

The tractor barn was secured by the same method as the horse barn—a wooden bar that slid across when a person wanted to open the double doors, and slid back when they wanted to keep them closed. Ben had to let go of Molly while he pushed the bar aside, and he could swear he heard her teeth chattering, even with the scarf covering her mouth.

He hoped, after braving the cold, she'd like his saddle and feel good about having seen it. Tramping out here tonight was a lot of trouble, particularly if the saddle turned out to be anticlimactic.

The tractor barn wasn't wired for electricity, which meant no heat and no lights. Once they were inside and he'd pulled the doors shut, the air was marginally warmer, but not by much. He reached into his pocket, but before he could turn on his flashlight app, she'd pulled off one mitten and activated hers.

She tugged her scarf down from her nose and mouth. "That was intense." Her words came out in little puffs of condensed vapor.

"And we have to do it all over again when we go back." More clouds fogged the air between them.

"I didn't say I didn't like it. Challenges are fun for me." Mist from their conversation hung between them.

"Me, too, actually." He'd felt a sense of kinship when she'd said that. Not everyone welcomed challenges in their life. He thought it was the only way a person could grow. "Shine your light along the floor so we don't trip over anything as we walk back there."

"Thank you for bringing me." She held the light steady as they walked to the back of the tractor barn.

In warm weather the place probably smelled of gas and oil, but freezing temperatures cancelled out most of the odor. Ben caught faint whiffs of the metallic scent of machinery, but it was subtle. Light from the phone allowed him to see the hulking forms of tractors. In the dark the barn *was* a little spooky.

He couldn't imagine sending her out here by herself, even if she would have been perfectly safe. Maybe her size made him feel protective, but he thought it was more than that. He loved her enthusiasm for new experiences, but having someone around as backup wasn't a bad idea. He'd never want to suggest she wasn't capable of anything she put her mind to, but if he could provide a safety net, that would be okay, too.

And what a ridiculous idea that was! He didn't expect to see her after she left the state on Monday. She had a lifetime of adventures ahead of her and he wouldn't be a part of any of them. So he could stop fantasizing about his role in her life, because he had none.

"To the right," he said as they neared the back of the barn. "Over in the corner. Lift the light a little. See that thing over there with the blanket covering it? That's the saddle. Hold the light steady."

She did as he asked and he noted that she was excellent at following directions when the situation required it. Stepping into the glow of her phone light, he grabbed two corners of the blanket and pulled. He considered making it even more dramatic by whipping it aside like a magician revealing his completed trick. But that would be showing off, and he wasn't into showing off.

"Oh, Ben."

The awe in her voice thrilled him. "Glad you like it." He turned toward her.

She was in shadow with her flashlight trained on the saddle. "I don't just *like* it. I *love* it." She moved forward and angled the light as she examined the saddle more closely. "Rosie Padgett was right. You're an artist."

"I don't know about that." Good thing he was in shadow, too, so she wouldn't see him blush. Later, when he was alone, he'd savor those words, but at the moment they made him uncomfortable.

"Then you underestimate yourself."

"I think of an artist as being somebody like Leonardo da Vinci, not Ben Radcliffe, saddlemaker."

"Then maybe your definition is a little too narrow." She traced the tooling on the saddle's fender. "Did you copy this design from somewhere? Is that why you don't feel like an artist?"

"No, I made it up."

"There you go. This is original art. It happens to be on a working saddle instead of on the wall of a museum, but personally, I like the idea of art in everyday life. Useful art. You took something that serves a function and made it beautiful. Like Grecian urns. They were made to be used, but that didn't keep the potters from decorating them with amazing pictures and turning them into works of art we study today."

"I guess."

"Listen to a history professor. If Sarah takes good care of it and passes it down, it could someday end up in a museum as an example of Western art."

"I think that's going a little far." Even though the barn was very cold, he was growing warmer by the minute. No one had ever said such things to him. He didn't believe a word of it, but that didn't mean he didn't like hearing it. "I've never studied art, really. I took an art class in high school because it was an easy A, but that doesn't mean—"

"Be quiet, Ben." She caressed the saddle one last time and turned back to him, the light moving with her. "Where are you? Oh, I see you." She walked over to him until she was standing inches away. "What was that you said when we were inside? That you liked me?"

"I said, that, yeah."

"And I asked you to elaborate. Would you care to do that now?" She kept the light trained on the floor.

That meant she was still mostly in shadow, and she was still bundled up like someone about to ski the Alps. But he sensed something in the air, a yearning that matched his own. "Instead of trying to explain it," he said, "maybe I should show you."

"Show me how?"

"Like this." Tossing his hat onto the saddle horn, he gathered her into his arms. She squeaked in surprise, but when he located her mouth, her squeak turned into a sigh. Oh, yeah. She wanted this as much as he did.

6

AT FIRST BEN'S lips were cold, but Molly's weren't. She'd had them covered with a scarf. Warming his lips took no time at all. After the first shock of discovering he was going to kiss her, she threw herself into the experience with abandon.

Rising to her toes, she wound her arms around his neck and gave it all she had. So did he, and oh, my goodness. A harmonica player knew what it was all about. She'd never kissed one before, but she hoped to be doing a lot more of this with Ben.

Although she'd never thought of a kiss as being creative, this one was. He caressed her lips so well and so thoroughly that she forgot the cold and the late hour. She forgot they were standing in a cavernous tractor barn surrounded by heavy equipment.

She even forgot that she wasn't in the habit of kissing men she'd known for mere hours. Come to think of it, she'd never done that. But everything about this kiss, from his coffee-and-dessert-flavored taste to his talented tongue, felt perfect.

As far as she was concerned, the kiss could go on

forever. Well, maybe not. The longer they kissed, the heavier they breathed. His hot mouth was making her light-headed in more ways than one.

That was her excuse for dropping her phone on the concrete floor. It hit with a sickening crack, but in her current aroused state, she didn't really care.

Ben pulled back, though, and gulped for air. "I think that was your phone."

"I think so, too." She dragged in a couple of quick breaths. "Kiss me some more."

With a soft groan, he lowered his head and settled his mouth over hers. This time he took the kiss deeper and invested it with a meaning she understood quite well. Intellectually she was shocked, but physically she was completely on board. The stroke of his tongue delivered a message, one she received with a rush of moisture that dampened her panties.

This time when he eased away from her, she was trembling. Like a swimmer breaking the surface, she gasped. Then she clutched his head and urged him back down. She wanted him to kiss her until the voice of caution stopped yelling at her that it was too soon to feel like this about him. "More."

He resisted, but he was panting and obviously as hot as she was. "This is crazy. I think we broke your phone. The light's out."

"We don't need light."

"That's not the point."

"Yes, it is. Come back here and do what you were doing some more. I really like it."

His chuckle was a little strained. "Me, too." Apparently he had both a strong will and a strong neck, because he held himself away from her. "But I can do a better job of it in a warm house, plus then we can check out your phone."

"I don't care about the damned phone." She sighed. "Which is a measure of how you affect me if I'm unconcerned about my techie toy."

"I'm flattered."

"I hope you're also turned on."

"That, too." He sounded amused.

"You realize the minute we step out into that Arctic air we'll lose momentum." And she'd begin to question the wisdom of sleeping with him. She just knew it.

His gloved hand brushed her cheek. "Speak for yourself. The way I'm feeling right now, I could make love to you on an ice floe."

She shivered, and it had nothing to do with the cold and everything to do with picturing them naked and going for it on any available flat surface. Oh, boy. She was actually considering having sex with a guy she'd just met.

As the power of his kisses faded a little, her conscience resumed its tedious lecture about her wanton behavior. She tried not to listen, but it was no use. "Maybe we should lose momentum." She said it with regret, but her conscience applauded. "How long have we known each other?"

He was silent for a moment. "Yeah, you're right. For the record, I don't ordinarily move this fast."

"I *never* move this fast. I go through the normal steps—coffee date, lunch date, dinner date." More smug applause from her conscience.

"So we skipped a couple of steps."

"It's not just the steps." Her conscience was in full control, now. "It's the time between the steps, when you talk on the phone with someone, when you have moments to contemplate them when they're not around, when you begin to miss them if you don't see them for a couple of days."

He took a shaky breath. "I know you're right, but we don't have that kind of time. You'll be gone in a few days."

She noticed he still hadn't let go of her. She could wiggle out of his arms, but she didn't want to do that. "You make a valid point." *Take that, conscience!* "I've never met anyone special when I was on vacation. My dating steps work great in Prescott, but this isn't quite that situation."

"Same here. I've never been bowled over by somebody who's about to leave town. Guess I don't know how to handle—"

"Bowled over? Really?" Her conscience was speechless at that.

"Yeah." There was a smile in his voice. "Really. That little pirouette you did for me after I took the dental floss out of your hair knocked me out."

"Wow. No one's ever told me I bowled them over." And if she needed justification for ignoring her dating steps, this might do the trick.

"Surprised the hell out of me, too. You're not my type at all."

"Oh? In what way?"

"Uh…the women I date are usually more…full-figured."

With an internal sigh, she decided this cozy embrace was over and pushed against his broad chest. "Then maybe you're hot for me because, even though I'm not your type, I'm handy and you're in the mood."

"Hey, hey, I didn't mean it like that." His arms tightened around her.

"Let me go, Ben. I get the picture. Chances are you'd be disappointed once our clothes are off, which they won't be, because I'd sooner strip in front of a grizzly than you."

"Let me say my piece, okay? Then if you want to stay away from me for the rest of your visit, I won't bother you."

Curiosity had always been both a blessing and a curse in her life. "Go ahead."

"You're right about what I've always considered my type of woman." He rubbed the small of her back while he talked.

"Centerfold worthy." She tried not to be affected by his touch. Logically she shouldn't feel it much through her bulky coat, but when it came to Ben, she was extra sensitive. "I'm not built to those specs."

"You don't have to be. You have something more important."

"Here it comes. You even said it already. You like that I have brains, but trust me, women don't want to be adored just for their brains, even if they think they do. They want to be worshipped for their bodies, even skinny ladies like me."

His voice grew husky. "You have no idea how much I want to do that, Molly."

"Because you've been through a long dry spell?"

"No, I haven't. I broke up with somebody a couple of months ago."

"For some guys, two months is a long time. You could be one of those guys."

"I could, but I'm not. It wasn't a very intense relationship, anyway." He kept rubbing her back with slow, sure strokes. "But you—you would be intense. I thought so before I kissed you, and now I know it for sure. You're so full of energy. That's very sexy."

"It is?" She was feeling a little better about being in his arms. A *lot* better, actually.

"Oh, yeah. You glow, Molly, and I'm so drawn to that. I want…" He swallowed. "I want to touch you all over and see if you'll glow even brighter. I bet you will." His voice roughened. "I want to see the excitement in your eyes when you're about to come. I want to see you go up in flames."

She gulped. And quivered. And decided that maybe her dating steps weren't all they were cracked up to be.

"That's all I have to say. If you want me to let you go and keep my distance while I'm here, I understand. We just met. I'm not a sexual opportunist, but you don't know me well enough to be convinced of that."

"Yes, I do." Her words were barely more than a whisper.

"You do?"

She cleared her throat. "Yes." She was smiling, but he wouldn't be able to see that. "A sexual opportunist wouldn't have announced I'm not his type."

He blew out a breath. "That was so lame of me. I'm sorry."

"Except you told me the truth."

"It was the truth until I met you. And besides that, you were insulted. I didn't mean to insult you." His sensual back rub continued. "Your body excites me in a way I can't describe very well."

"You're welcome to keep trying."

He chuckled. "Okay, let me see if I can come up

with a way to say it that makes sense. It's like you're sneaky sexy. A stealth vixen."

"A stealth vixen. I like that." She also liked the way he'd brought her closer until she was pressed tight against his warm body. Even with the layers between them, she knew for a fact he wasn't making this up. He really did want her.

"It's taken me awhile to evolve, but I think I'm finally learning to appreciate subtlety." He paused in midstroke. "How am I doing? Is any of this making sense?"

"Sort of."

"Where are we on your dating chart?"

"Is this your way of asking if I'll go to bed with you when we get back to the house?"

"I wish." He hugged her a little bit closer. "Much as I would love that, all we can do is fool around a little. No grand finale tonight, I'm afraid. I wasn't expecting this and I'm completely unprepared."

She had a genius IQ, but it didn't take a genius to figure out what he was talking about. She debated telling him what she knew and finally decided that keeping the information to herself might not be right. He should have all the facts, too.

Besides, she liked the idea of rocking him back on his heels. "Actually, that's not a problem."

His sharp intake of breath was gratifying. "Why not?"

"There's a box in your bathroom."

"You're kidding."

"I would never kid about a thing like that, Ben. That would be cruel."

"And you just happen to know this?"

"I had a headache yesterday and I forgot to bring aspirin. There wasn't any in my bathroom, so I looked in yours."

"I see."

Honesty made her amend that statement. "Actually, I found the aspirin right away, but once I was in there, I wondered what else was tucked in the drawers, so I checked everything out."

"God almighty, you're like a little cat, poking your nose in everywhere. And I love it." He hesitated. "But I'm still trying to get a bead on where we stand. Are we at yes, no or maybe?"

"We're at maybe. I still think we need to slow down a little. Don't you?"

"Truthfully? No. We're two consenting adults and what happens upstairs stays upstairs. We've both proven we can keep a secret, and we only have four nights before you leave. By denying ourselves tonight, we've taken a potentially great experience off the table."

"What if it doesn't go well?"

"Then I'll leave first thing Saturday morning. You'll only have to put up with me another twenty-four hours and I'll be gone." His voice dropped to a sexy murmur. "But it'll go well."

Her heart beat faster. "You're sure about that?"

"Yes." And he kissed her again.

The second his mouth covered hers, he proved that he knew what he was talking about. A man who could kiss like this, who could use his tongue with such devastating effect, a man who knew exactly the right angle for maximum pleasure—that man would bring the same originality and expertise to lovemaking. She'd be a fool to miss out on even one night of sharing his bed.

When he released her, he didn't let go right away, which was a good thing because she might have collapsed onto the cement floor. She was just that unsteady. Mentally, though, she was extremely focused on returning to the house. So much so that she forgot both the uncovered saddle and her dropped phone. "Let's go."

Laughter rippled in his voice. "First I have to cover the saddle."

"Oh. Right."

He turned on his flashlight app and aimed it at the floor. "And there's your phone."

"Thanks." She leaned down and picked it up. The screen was cracked, but the phone itself might be operational. She activated it. "Everything looks fine. I just need a new screen."

"Good." He took his hat off the saddle horn and put it on. "Would you please hold the light for me?"

"Sure." She tucked away her phone and took his. "It really is beautiful. Now I wish I'd had a chance to contribute to the fund, but my trip up here was kind of a last-minute decision. I'm sure Jack had it handled long before I arrived."

"He did." Ben arranged the blanket so the saddle was completely concealed. "He took up a collection back in October and gave me half my fee then." He turned back to her. "You mean you almost didn't make it here?"

"Almost. Christmas is special at Mom and Dad's house, and I usually spend the first part of my Christmas break helping cook and decorate. Plus the weather's dicey this time of year. Originally I planned to wait until summer."

"Then we wouldn't have met."

"Probably not."

"What made you change your mind and come before Christmas?"

"Aunt Sarah's birthday party tomorrow, for one thing, but then she told me about this set of diaries that her mother-in-law, Nelsie Chance, had kept for years. I was very eager to read them, which I have, and they're wonderful. I even found mention of me in there. But I could have put that off until next summer, too. I just had this hunch that I should come up here now, for some reason."

"Hmm." He adjusted the fit of his Stetson. "Listen, do you think…" Then he shook his head. "Never mind. I don't believe in that stuff."

"What stuff?"

"Fate, kismet, that kind of thing."

She didn't say anything because she *did* believe in it and was beginning to wonder if her hunch had been about him. But she wasn't ready to announce that thought. She might never admit it to him. So much depended on how the next few days went for them. Or the next few hours.

But apparently he was over there interpreting her silence. "You believe in it, don't you?"

"A little."

"Well, I don't."

That made her smile. He was the one who'd brought it up in the first place, but she wouldn't point that out to him. The instant attraction between them excited him, but it probably made him nervous, too.

Not surprising. It made *her* nervous. Going to bed with him tonight was so far out of her comfort zone it was in the next zip code. But that didn't mean she'd decided not to. She was still thinking.

7

As THEY HURRIED from the tractor barn back to the house, Ben still wasn't clear on whether Molly wanted to have sex with him or not. She hadn't specifically said she would, but her kiss certainly tasted like yes.

Yet he should probably give her a little more information before they took that step. Her dreams had to include a family of her own, but all he could share would be this brief time with her. Then he'd bow out of her life.

She didn't realize that, and he should be straight with her before anything happened between them. Someday she'd settle down with a man who wanted a family, but in the meantime, here they were, crazy for each other. If she was willing to share her warmth for a long weekend, he'd take it.

On the porch they quietly brushed off the snow that clung to their jackets. The porch stretched the length of the house, and according to Jack, rockers lined it during the summer. If Ben came back this summer for Calamity Sam, he'd make a point to enjoy some time in a rocker and take in the view of the Tetons.

Molly wouldn't be here, though. A tug at his heart told him that he'd miss her cheerful presence. He'd have to get over that, because she was most definitely not for him, not for the long haul, anyway.

But now, as he carefully opened the door hung with a giant pine wreath, he thought maybe she could be his for a little while. While they wordlessly removed their boots and set them on a mat by the front door, he thought about what he wanted to say to her. He didn't relish giving a full explanation, but he had to tell her this wasn't a lead-in to something more.

That was assuming she would consider sharing his bed. As they climbed the stairs to the second floor, he unbuttoned his coat. Then he grabbed her by the hand before she could start back to her room. "Molly."

She turned toward him, her eyes bright and her skin flushed.

"You know I want you."

"Yes." She swallowed. "And I—"

"There's something you need to know about me." He took a deep breath. "Saying this might seem weird, except…you're so into family, and I'm…not."

Her expression grew thoughtful. "Okay."

"I never plan to have kids. I'm not even sure if I'll ever get married." He wondered if she'd laugh and say the topic was premature. Or maybe she'd ask him why he felt that way.

Instead, her gaze softened. "Thank you for telling me."

"Seemed like the right thing." And he'd probably ruined his chances, but at least he'd be able to live with himself. "I guess that's that, then." But he didn't let go of her hand, just in case he hadn't blown it with her.

A smile touched the corners of her mouth. "Giving up?"

His heart kicked into high gear. "I thought maybe, under the circumstances, you'd rather—"

"You thought wrong."

"Thank God." Watching the glow of anticipation return to her eyes made his body hum.

"But first I should probably..." She gestured toward her bedroom.

"You don't need anything. Come with me." He wasn't about to lose momentum now. He tugged her down the hallway. "First stop, the bathroom."

She started laughing.

"Hey, you know where they are. I could waste precious time looking for them."

"You're incorrigible."

He'd never been with a woman whose vocabulary included *incorrigible.* He liked it more than he would have believed. He hadn't realized that smart women turned him on. Maybe before this episode ended, he'd make love to her while she wore the glasses she loved so much.

She located the box of condoms and lobbed them in his direction. "Don't say I never did anything for you."

He caught them in one hand. "I'd never say that, not in a million years." Taking her by the hand again, he led her into the bedroom and nudged the door closed with one foot.

Reluctant to break the magical connection between them, he tossed the box of condoms on the nearest nightstand. Coordination came in handy sometimes. Then he sent his hat sailing toward the bedpost and was gratified when he scored a ringer.

"Impressive."

"That's nothing." Pulling her into his arms, he plucked off her knit cap. Her hair was another glorious thing about her, and he combed his fingers through it, marveling at the many shades of color caught in the lamplight. "Cowboys are known for their agility. I can have you naked in ten seconds flat."

Her green eyes flashed. "Only if I cooperate."

"Please cooperate." He unwound the red scarf and dropped it to the floor. "I'm a desperate man."

"In that case…" She unzipped her parka and shrugged out of it. "I wouldn't want to be responsible for causing undue stress."

"Now I'm a grateful man." He got a firm grip on the hem of her sweater and tugged it over her head. He'd expected a utilitarian bra underneath. Instead she wore a lacy black number that made him catch his breath.

She stepped back with a coy smile. "When a girl doesn't have much to show off, she goes for the prettiest underwear she can find. Allow me." She reached behind her back.

The action thrust her pert breasts forward, and his mouth went dry. Then she unfastened the clasp and slowly drew the wisp of black lace away from the sweetest breasts he'd ever seen. He reached out.

"Not yet." She backed away another step. "You're falling behind."

He'd been so eager to get her out of her clothes that he'd lost track of the fact he still wore everything but his hat. He tossed the scarf aside and took off his sheepskin jacket.

"Give it here."

"You want my jacket?"

"I've always wondered what sheepskin would feel like on my bare skin." She draped his jacket over her shoulders and wrapped it around her. "Nice." Turning her cheek, she rubbed it against the soft collar. "Smells like you."

Transfixed by the sight of her stroking her cheek with his jacket lining, he stood motionless in the middle of the room.

"You're still behind, cowboy."

And so he was. He unfastened the cuffs of his Western shirt and the snaps down the front popped in rapid succession as he wrenched it open. In no time he'd dropped it to the floor. "Better?"

Her gaze moved from his face to his chest and the heat in those green eyes told him all he needed to know. This would be quite an evening. He'd closed the door, but now he wondered if he should stuff a towel under it to further soundproof the room.

At least Sarah and Pete slept downstairs at the opposite end of the house. He hoped that created enough distance to muffle what could become a noisy interlude.

"Now you're the one who's behind." His voice sounded rusty. "You're wearing my jacket."

"I like it."

His first impulse was to tell her she could have it, but that would be stupid for many reasons, most of them centering on the impermanence of this arrangement. "I'm glad. Now drop it."

She allowed the jacket to slide from her shoulders onto the floor. It was one of the most seductive maneuvers he'd ever seen. Once it was gone, she shoved her hands in the back pockets of her jeans, thrust her breasts forward and lifted her chin. "Now what?"

He lost it. With a groan of pure lust, he eliminated the distance between them and cupped her breasts in both hands. Then he leaned down and kissed her hard. She kissed him right back, rising on her toes and gripping his shoulders for balance.

Her breasts felt perfect in his hands and her throaty moans told him how much she loved having him touch her there. He stroked her silken skin and his cock thickened. Beneath his palms, her nipples hardened in arousal. He pinched them lightly and she moaned again, louder this time.

Wrenching her mouth from his and struggling for breath, she gazed up at him. Her words came out in a rush. "Take me to bed, now. Please."

He didn't have to be asked twice. Sliding his hands under her firm bottom, he lifted her up. She was light as a sunbeam and twice as warm. When she wrapped her legs around his waist, he felt the heat coming from her core, and the crotch of her jeans was damp. Hallelujah.

Carrying her to the bed, he set her on the edge of the mattress so he could pull off her jeans and panties. She was so finely made, so delicate. As he caressed each new treasure he uncovered, he also found out just how hot and wet she was, how breathless with desire.

He dropped to his knees, eager to give pleasure to a woman who was so ready for it.

"Not now." She cradled his head in both hands, her fingers gripping him tight, her gaze intense. "I ache, Ben. I've never ached like this. I need you inside me."

So he stood and backed away as she stretched out on the comforter. He hadn't bothered to pull it down.

There was no need. The room was warm and about to get a whole lot warmer.

She turned her head to watch as he stripped off the rest of his clothes and freed his aching cock. Her eyes widened. "Oh, my."

For the first time, he worried that he'd be too much for her. If he hurt her, even a little bit, he'd never forgive himself. His voice tight with lust, he sought to reassure her. "I'll take it slow."

She swallowed. "Okay."

His blood pounded in his ears. "Don't worry. You'll be in charge."

"Oh." Her rapid breathing made her breasts tremble invitingly. "That's good." A tiny smile touched her kiss-reddened lips and a gleam lit her green eyes.

"I guess you like that idea. Big surprise." His hands shook as he rolled on a condom. He didn't need it for birth control, but he didn't care to get into that discussion.

He didn't care to get into *any* discussion. She craved relief and by God, so did he. Neither of them needed conversation. He'd never wanted a woman so much, which meant he had to watch himself or he'd take her with all the force of that wanting. She might be a tough little thing with a will of iron, but she was no match for him if he allowed his passion free rein.

He paused before putting a knee on the bed and took a shaky breath. "Scoot over," he said softly. "So I can lie on my back. That's how we'll do this."

She followed his directions and propped her chin on her fist to watch him as he settled down beside her. "So I'm in charge?"

"Completely."

She looked him up and down, and her gaze lingered on his cock, which projected upward with the rigidity of a sundial. "Oh, boy."

That's when he realized he was in for it. He hadn't intended for this to be a test of his control, but now it likely would be. The other part of wanting her so much was that he felt as if he could come any minute. That would be bad on many levels.

She wasted no time scrambling to her knees and straddling his thighs. Then she sat there, her bare bottom warm against his skin as she contemplated him, her cheeks flushed. "I need you so much, but you are *huge.*"

He resisted the urge to grab her and lift her into position. With the entrance to nirvana so very close, yet so very far, his brain was on tilt. "You don't have to take it all." But how he hoped she could.

"I want to." She wrapped her fingers around his latex-covered cock.

He shuddered. "Then…just try." *Dear God, please try, before I go out of my effing mind.*

Slowly she rose on her knees and leaned over to flatten her hands on his chest. Her hair tumbled over her shoulders in waves of abandon. "Hold still."

"Right." His breathing roughened and he fisted his hands at his sides.

"Here goes nothing." She closed her eyes in concentration while she shifted her hips. Eventually, after what seemed like forever, she pressed the blunt tip of his cock right where it needed to be for the next stage.

He swore under his breath as her slick heat taunted him almost beyond endurance.

"Mmm." She looked into his eyes. "Ready?"

"Hell, yeah."

She eased down a little and sucked in air.

"Too much?"

"Oh, no." She moaned softly and took him slightly deeper. "This is…amazing. I thought it might be, and now…now…"

He didn't dare speak. He was too busy going through his multiplication tables and naming the U.S. presidents while he fought off his climax. She picked up another inch of real estate and he started counting backward from a hundred by threes.

Although he'd been worried that he'd be too big for her, he hadn't contemplated the flipside of that. He hadn't considered that her tight sheath would intensify the friction for him, too. He was thinking about it now as she continued her slow downward journey and he forgot how to breathe.

She also wasn't quiet about her plan to take all he had to give. She heralded each bit of progress with heartfelt moans and blissful sighs, which made it even tougher for him to stay in control. Then her core muscles clenched.

He drew in a sharp breath and glared at her. "Don't."

"I can't…help it." Her eyes were dark with excitement. "Nothing has ever felt…" She gasped as she settled further down. "Like this."

He lifted his head to gauge her progress. That was a mistake. The visual of his cock almost completely buried except for a mere inch sent a spasm through him. He groaned and fought against coming.

"I'm going for it." Taking a ragged breath, she moved the rest of the way and erupted, her climax rolling over his cock as her wild cries filled the room.

That wiped out his last ounce of control and he arched upward, claiming whatever fraction remained with a deep bellow of satisfaction as he came. *Yes, oh, yes!* Her tight channel clenched as he withdrew and thrust again. Pleasure pulsed through him in a dizzying spiral that left him gulping for air.

He couldn't say how long the moment lasted. He lost all track of time as he lay immersed in the incredible sensation of coming inside Molly Gallagher. When she slid down to rest her cheek on his damp chest, he finally allowed himself to hold her.

Until then he'd been true to his promise that she was in charge, but now he felt safe wrapping her in his arms. She relaxed against him, and her weight was no more than that of a pillow. The top of her head only reached his chin and her waist wasn't much bigger than his thigh. Yet she'd taken his cock deep into her body and treated it to the best time of its life.

"I loved that," she murmured.

"Me, too."

"Next time you can be in charge."

He smiled and combed her tousled hair with his fingers. "So you want to do this again?"

She laughed softly. "I do. And now that I know we fit, I'll let you direct the action."

Normally he required some recovery time. Apparently not with this woman. All she had to do was say she wanted more, and his body was willing to give her what she wanted.

8

WHILE BEN LEFT the room to dispose of the condom, Molly got under the covers and snuggled down to savor the most satisfying orgasm of her life. And she'd had it with an honorable man who'd admitted he was the wrong guy for her. She wanted to know why he'd decided against having a family, but something told her the reasons were extremely private.

Funny, but even though they'd just had great sex, she didn't feel as if she knew him well enough to pry into his personal business. He'd given her the truth, and she admired him for doing that much. They only had a short time together, and that might not be long enough for him to let down his guard. She wouldn't push, either.

Instead, she'd be grateful for this amazing experience, although she didn't know whether Ben was good in bed or not. Maybe with a package like his, he didn't have to try very hard to make a woman extremely happy.

He did, however, have to be gentle if the lady in question was built the way she was. She'd been intimidated when he'd first unveiled that bad boy, but intrigued and curious. Besides that, his kisses had aroused her to the point of no return, and although he'd offered oral sex to begin with, she'd wanted the full-body experience. She just hadn't realized how full he'd make her feel.

They hadn't moved much. They hadn't needed to. But she'd like to find out how a little movement would work out for them. She'd put his restraint to the ultimate test, and he'd controlled himself admirably. After that go-round, she didn't have to worry that he'd forget himself and take her too hard or too fast.

His consideration and tenderness said a great deal about him. He'd stockpiled some trust while holding himself motionless as she slowly discovered whether she could accommodate him. Putting him in charge didn't scare her a bit.

It aroused the hell out of her, though. He was by far the most exciting man she'd ever had sex with. When he walked back in the room, closing the door behind him, she sat up. "Could you just stand there for a minute and let me look at you?"

He grinned. "So I'm not in charge, after all?"

"You are, but once you climb into this bed, I won't get the same view as I have now."

"All right." He stayed where he was.

She took her time surveying his powerful chest sprinkled with dark hair before moving lower to his abs.

He shifted his weight. "You know what? Fair is fair. Throw back the covers so I can look at you."

She did, although she couldn't believe her body would affect him the way his affected her. The soft sheen of lamplight on his broad shoulders made her moist and achy. And when she gazed upon the equipment that could relieve that ache…

Hello. Maybe her body held the power to arouse him, after all. As his dark eyes focused on her, his penis, looking as impressive as it had the first time, rose from its base of dark curls.

"See what you do to me?" His voice was a soft caress.

She nodded. Her body quivered as he walked over to the bed and brought all that wonderfulness with him.

"It's not nearly as easy for me to see what I do to you." He sat on the edge of the bed and cupped one of her breasts in his hand. "Your nipples tell me a little something." He brushed his thumb over the one that was most accessible.

She moaned and arched into the caress.

"That tells me you like me to touch you." His thumb flicked her nipple in a lazy rhythm.

"Yes." Her blood heated.

"Now your skin is flushed, which tells me you're becoming excited." His glance roamed over her. "But in order to find out exactly how much you want me, I have to investigate further." Leaning forward, he nibbled on her mouth. "Spread your legs for me, Molly. Let me explore."

Heart pounding, she opened her thighs. He continued to give her teasing little kisses and nips as he slid his hand down over her stomach, tunneled through her curls and found what he was looking for.

"Ah, Molly." He probed her with knowing fingers. "Now I know how much you want me." He stroked deep.

Without warning, her body tightened around his fingers. She gasped at the sudden onslaught of an impending orgasm.

His soft chuckle tickled her mouth. "You're ready now, aren't you, sweet lady?" He pumped his fingers back and forth. "You're going to come for me in a minute or two, aren't you?"

She had no words for him, only whimpers as he increased the pace, curving his fingers and thrusting with devastating skill. The rhythmic, liquid sound of his moving fingers made the caress even more erotic. She lifted her hips, wanting deeper, wanting more.

"That's my girl. Take what you want. Ask for it." He slipped his arm behind her hips, supporting her as he worked his magic.

She'd wondered if he was really good in bed. He was giving her the answer. Maybe she should be embarrassed by how easily he'd seduced her with his words and his touch. But she didn't have time to be embarrassed.

She didn't have time for anything but this…letting go…coming apart…coming…crying out his name— over and over and over as he coaxed a shattering response from her willing body.

At last, panting and quivering, she sank back to the mattress and looked up at him, dazed by her own abandon.

He smiled. "I knew you'd be like this." Slowly he withdrew his hand and trailed his moist fingers up her body.

The brush of his fingers over her hot skin ignited the fire again. It burned low, but it still burned. She swallowed. "Like how?"

"Eager. Responsive. Sensual. Easily aroused. I shouldn't take advantage of that. I should let you rest, but…" He reached for the box of condoms. "Once more, Molly. Then we'll sleep."

She doubted that once more would be enough, at least for her. He was a powerful aphrodisiac. The memory of his thick penis filling her brought back the familiar ache deep in her core.

"You have such an expressive face." He tore open the packet. "You don't agree with my plan, do you?"

She shrugged. "Why set limits?"

"Because I think you need to get used to me." He rolled on the condom.

"So you say."

"I'm not taking any chances." He moved over her. "Our nights together should be nothing but pleasure. No pain." Grabbing a pillow from the other side of the bed, he lifted her easily and tucked it under her hips. "That's better. Now, bend your knees."

If he hadn't already loved her so thoroughly, she might have been shocked at the way he pushed her knees back and opened her to his gaze. But then he nudged her with his penis, and as he pushed slowly inside, she understood. He'd positioned her so that she could take him in this way, too.

And, oh, it was heaven. When he stopped halfway, she moaned in protest. "More."

"Give me a second or two." He clenched his jaw and lowered his head. "You tempt me to come like no one ever has."

"I do?" She liked that.

"You fit me like a glove." His chest heaved. "A

smooth, velvet glove that's been warmed by the fire. The deeper I go, the better it gets."

His description turned her on even more, making her voice husky. "For me, too."

"I thought maybe the second time would be...less intense." He shuddered and gazed at her with eyes filled with lust. "I think it's more, not less."

"You can come." She felt her own response building fast. "You don't have to hold back for my sake."

He gave her a crooked smile. "It's not for your sake. It's for mine." He took another ragged breath. "Okay. Moving on." He eased forward slowly and paused again. "You all right?"

"Never better." She tingled all over, and deep inside, her womb tightened in response to the glide of his penis. "Keep going."

"I don't want to hurt you."

"You won't. You fit, remember?"

"Oh, I remember, Molly. I remember *this*." He groaned and pushed home.

She sucked in a breath. So did he, and it was glorious. He wouldn't have to do another thing, and she could reach orgasm just because he was locked tight against all the places that needed contact. All she had to do was squeeze a little bit...

"Molly." Her name was an urgent warning. "Ah, hell, I have to move or go crazy. Hang on."

She clutched his shoulders because they were within reach. No sooner had she grabbed hold of him than he groaned and began to thrust, slowly at first, then more rapidly.

"Tell me..." He panted as he increased the pace yet

again, lifting her off the bed with each forward motion of his hips. "Tell me if it hurts. I'll stop."

"No!" She was on the wildest ride of her life and loving it. "Don't stop!" If she was sore later, she didn't care.

The headboard thumped against the wall in an ever-faster rhythm until he plunged into her with a cry that was half groan, half growl. His last surge tipped her over the edge, and as he pulsed within her, she came with a long, wailing cry of release, pleasure and total surrender.

All movement stopped as the room filled with the sound of their tortured breathing.

"Oh, Molly." He gulped in air. "I'm so sorry."

"Don't you dare be sorry!"

He leaned his forehead against hers. "But I lost control. I swore I wouldn't do that."

She struggled to breathe. "Because I made you, right?"

"Yes. No! I should be able to—"

"I'm too powerful."

Slowly he lifted his head and gazed down at her. Then a slow smile turned into a low chuckle. "Yeah. You are small but mighty. I'm a helpless servant who worships at your feet."

"Or sometimes a little higher."

"Whenever I can get away with it." He searched her expression. "Are you really okay?"

"Yes."

"Would you tell me if you weren't?"

"Of course. That was incredible. I've never had sex like that."

"Me, either." He leaned down and kissed her gently. "Thank you. I'll be right back. Don't go away."

"I have no intention of going away. Not after a performance like that."

"We're sleeping after this, just so you know." Easing away from her, he left the bed. But as he started out of the room, he paused and swore. It wasn't an angry response, just an irritated one.

She couldn't imagine what had made him react like that. "Is something wrong?" She sat up.

"Not really. No worries." He left the room quickly.

She thought about the incident until he came back. Only one thing explained his behavior, and if she was right about what had happened, she needed to know about it.

When he returned, she was ready for him. "Ben, did the condom break?"

His expression gave her the answer.

"That's what I thought." Her mind sorted through the options. She'd never been in this position before, but she'd figure it out. "I think we need to—"

"We don't need to do anything."

"That's not exactly true. We just met, so pregnancy wouldn't be a good thing under the circumstances. I—"

"You won't get pregnant."

She didn't appreciate his cavalier attitude. "You don't know that. My family is extremely fertile. They get pregnant like that." She snapped her fingers.

"I've had a vasectomy."

She had her mouth open to offer more arguments for treating this as a serious situation, but she closed it and stared at him. "I guess you *really* don't want kids."

"No."

She waited to see if he'd elaborate. He didn't, which told her she'd guessed right. This was a sensitive topic. "I guess you wore the condom for health reasons."

"No. My last girlfriend was a nurse. She wouldn't go to bed with any guy unless he had a clean bill of health. Once she found out about my vasectomy, she was thrilled that we didn't have to use anything."

"Oh." The thought of him having sex with another woman didn't sit well with her, but that wasn't the issue here. "Were you worried about me?"

"Of course not. I'm sure you're squeaky clean."

She was, but that wasn't the issue, either. "So why didn't you suggest we go without?" He'd been willing to have this frank discussion with another woman, after all.

"Partly because we'd just met, and it's one of those lame things guys try to get away with."

"You thought I wouldn't believe you."

"Right."

"Why did your last girlfriend believe you?"

He sighed and walked over to sit on the side of the bed. Then he took her hand in his. He laced his fingers through hers but didn't look at her. "Because I told her why I'd gotten a vasectomy."

"Then please tell me."

"I think it's a little harder to tell you."

That hurt. "Do I come across as judgmental? If so, I don't mean to."

He looked into her eyes. "You come across as someone who's known nothing but loving kindness all her life. I hate the idea of bringing ugliness into that world. Maddie wasn't like that. She was…I guess you could say she was jaded. Oddly enough, that was why I broke up with her. She was too cynical and that began to bother me."

"Oh, Ben." Heart breaking for him, she cupped his cheek and searched his gaze. "What in God's name has happened to you?"

"Let's just say I didn't have your upbringing, and I'm afraid I might repeat that pattern. I can't risk it."

She thought he probably was wrong about himself, but he might not believe her if she said so. She could also sense that he didn't want to talk about his past and how it had shaped him.

"Ah, Molly." He lifted their clasped hands and kissed her fingertips. "You feel so absolutely right, but I wonder if I'm being selfish. I can't offer you any of the things you want."

"That's not entirely true."

"Sex doesn't count."

"Who says?"

"I do." He touched her cheek. "You'll find someone who'll give you great sex and lots of babies."

She squeezed his hand. "Fine. I'll keep an eye out for that person. But in the meantime, could I please have more great sex with you? Because I really like how you do it."

9

BEN DIDN'T KNOW a guy in the world who could refuse a request like that. Besides, after two climaxes, he had the staying power to make long, slow love to Molly. She seemed to like that as much as she'd liked the wall-banging kind.

Turned out, so did he. A whole hell of a lot, in fact. Afterward, he gathered her close and they drifted off to sleep in each other's arms.

He woke up before she did, experiencing an emotion that didn't come often to him. At first he had trouble naming it, but finally he settled on the description that seemed to fit. He was contented.

The reason was easy to figure out. He'd enjoyed amazing sex with a woman he liked well enough to sleep with in the literal sense. He hardly ever woke up with a woman. Usually he went to their place and left that same night. Staying for breakfast gave the wrong impression, as if he might be considering a more permanent arrangement.

But he and Molly had put everything on the table, or enough that she understood why he wasn't the one for her. He didn't have to dredge up the past and talk about his crummy family or his fears about turning into his dad.

Instead, they could enjoy each other and part ways as friends. If he didn't want to think about the leaving right now, so what? Philosophers said that the trick to happiness was staying in the moment, so he'd do that. And in this moment, he was extremely happy. He couldn't remember being happier, in fact.

He could faintly smell cookies baking and the muted sound of people talking on the floor below. It must be after seven if the cookies were already in the oven. He still cradled Molly against the curve of his body, his arm tucked around her waist. She'd wanted to be part of the cookie situation, but setting an alarm had been the last thing on his mind and probably on hers.

No surprise that they'd overslept. They'd worn each other out, in a good way. He'd love to stay like this a little longer, but she might not thank him for it.

He murmured her name.

She stirred in his arms and yawned.

So cute, that little yawn. Funny how his feelings for her were more tender than lustful this morning. "If you still want to bake cookies, you need to get up."

"Cookies!" She scrambled to a sitting position and stared at him in dismay. "I forgot the cookies!"

"Sorry. Me, too."

"It's okay. Not your fault, but I have to boogie." She left the bed, gathered up her clothes, and began tugging them on. "Thank you for a wonderful night."

He propped himself up on his elbow. "You're welcome. Doing anything special tonight after the party?"

"I hope so."

"Would it happen to involve coming back here?"

She laughed. "Yes, unless you'd rather come to my room where we'd probably end up falling off the double bed."

"No, thanks. I'll meet you back here in about..." He glanced over at the small clock on the nightstand. "About eighteen hours, give or take."

"That's a long time."

"I know. Want to schedule a rendezvous in the middle of the day?"

After pulling her sweater over her head, she looked at him. "I'd love to, but I don't think we dare. The house will be full of people today. I'll be pretty busy, and besides, somebody might come up here. I wouldn't want them to hear us, or worse yet, walk in on us."

"Which brings up another important point. How do you want to play this?"

She was quiet for a little too long. "I don't know."

He couldn't blame her for being hesitant to reveal what was going on between them. She was a part of this family and her behavior would come under some scrutiny as a result. Even though she was an adult capable of making her own decisions, Sarah might feel a certain responsibility for her.

"We'll keep it to ourselves," he said, letting her off the hook.

"Thank you." Relief showed in her expression. "It's not that I'm ashamed of what we've done. It's just—"

"Never mind. I get it. You don't want your relatives to know you hopped into bed with a virtual stranger on his first night here."

"When you put it that way, it sounds pretty wild, doesn't it?"

He smiled. "It *was* pretty wild."

"Yeah." Her voice was filled with wonder, as if she couldn't quite believe what had happened in this room. "This is not like me, at all."

He sat up. "Regrets?" He said it lightly, but her answer meant more to him than he wanted to admit.

She met his gaze. "No. Last night was amazing. I didn't know sex could feel like that, or that I could respond the way I did. I'll never forget what we've shared."

"That sounds like a kiss-off speech." His chest felt tight. "Are you reconsidering meeting me after the party?"

"Oh, no, I want to."

He let out his breath.

"But last night I didn't give much thought to how our choice could be interpreted by the rest of the family. To be honest, I wasn't doing much thinking at all. I wanted you and that wiped out every other consideration."

"And now you're worried about what others might think."

"I am. Maybe that's cowardly and I should be stronger, but—"

"Hey, you don't have to explain." He was a little disappointed, but he did understand. Tossing back the covers, he searched the floor for his underwear. "I *am* a virtual stranger."

"Not anymore."

"Nobody else will find out." He located his briefs and pulled them on. "Not from me, anyway."

"Thank you, Ben."

"Just don't go ogling my butt or someone might notice."

"I promise not to ogle your butt, although I have to say, it's very ogle-worthy." She grabbed her boots and jacket. "So is the rest of you."

"Likewise." He stepped into his jeans.

"Don't be silly."

"I'm not being silly." After picking up his shirt, he glanced at her. "Your body drives me out of my mind."

"Come on. You don't have to say that."

"No, I don't, which is why I *am* saying it." He took a deep breath and let it out. His intense gaze locked with hers. "I look at you and think of how you rode my cock, your breasts bouncing, and how wet you are for me, always, and how tight, and how sliding inside you makes me want to come the minute we connect."

Her cheeks flushed.

"I won't be able to not think about that today, Molly."

She swallowed. "Me, either. So we'd better stay away from each other—at least, most of the time." With a little moan of frustration, she whirled toward the door. "I'm getting out of here while I still can."

"Check the hall and make sure the coast is clear."

"I will. Tonight I'll come over in my robe. That might help."

He chuckled. "It'll certainly make it easier to get started."

She glanced at the box of condoms on the nightstand. "Put that back, okay?"

"You bet."

Opening the door, she peered out. "Looks deserted." Then she turned and her gaze swept over him. "You're a beautiful man."

His throat tightened. "You're a beautiful woman."

She gave him a quick smile before running out into the hall.

He stepped to the door and watched until she disappeared into her room. Then he sighed. Although he wouldn't change a single thing that had happened, she was working her way under his skin. Eventually he'd have to face the truth—a long weekend with her wouldn't be nearly enough. But he wouldn't worry about that today. Today he would practice ignoring her. That would be challenge enough without thinking about a future that didn't have Molly in it.

10

MOLLY HAD NEVER thought of herself as much of an actress, but she hoped she gave a convincing performance as she moved through the day of party preparations. Ben made good on his offer to help, which meant he was tantalizingly close by most of the time. He moved furniture with ease and his height came in handy for attaching decorations to the exposed ceiling beams.

Not for the first time, she turned and found herself staring at his impressive package, which was currently at eye level while he stood on a ladder to hang a cluster of balloons and a Happy Birthday banner.

She hoped nobody had caught her sudden intake of breath or the blush she'd felt rising to her cheeks. Or maybe they'd think she was a modest little thing who wasn't used to getting up close and personal with a man endowed like Ben. Little did they know she knew all about what he kept tucked away inside his jeans.

The bustle of preparations helped to cover any slip-ups on her part. Holiday traditions at the Last Chance felt familiar to Molly, which wasn't surprising considering that her Grandpa Seth had been Nelsie's brother.

The Christmas carols blasting from the sound system in the living room were by the same artists Molly's family loved.

She was thrilled to arrange the nativity scene on the mantle. Her parents had an identical set that was also a little chipped, yet beloved. Nelsie had bought both sets more than seventy years ago and had given one to her brother and his wife.

Tasks like this temporarily distracted her from thinking about Ben. Each time she finished a chore, she'd turn around, and there he'd be, doing something helpful and manly. He was the most tempting man she'd ever met.

He treated her with casual courtesy, as if he barely noticed her. She had the perverse urge to pinch his butt and remind him that she was standing behind him as he showed off his perfect ass to every female in the vicinity.

That urge was so unfair. She was the one who'd been reluctant to let anyone know that they'd established an extremely intimate connection on a very brief acquaintance. He was only acting the way she'd asked him to.

Possessiveness on her part was not only unattractive but uncalled-for. They'd struck a deal—a fun romp for however long he was here followed by a cheerful parting of the ways. Under those circumstances, she had no claim on him, and he had no claim on her.

The arrangement felt completely unreal to her, though, because she'd never entered into one like it before. She'd never gone to bed with a man who hadn't been a potential mate. None of her three previous lovers had turned out to be her one and only, but she hadn't known that until they'd spent some quality time together, including having sex.

What she'd shared with them hadn't come within a mile of what she'd discovered with Ben, and now she had a whole new concept of what made for a perfect partner. She hoped that Ben wasn't one in a million. If so, she was in for a long search.

Molly arrived early for lunch in the big dining room. She sat down with Sarah and Pete, who were the only two at their table so far. Ben moved on past, as if heading for a spot on the other side of the room.

But Pete called out to him, and he turned back. "Come and sit with us," Pete said. "I had some more thoughts on your potential breeding program. You might be interested in one of our mares, as well."

Ben sat down next to Pete, across the table from Molly. "Don't know if I can afford that, yet."

"Maybe we could work out a deal. Time payments, or first look at the foal. There are all sorts of creative ways to do it. Jack and I talked and we want to help in any way we can."

Ben nodded. "That's good to know. Where is Jack, anyway?"

"Josie had an emergency at the bar. A pipe broke, so he's helping her handle it."

"I've heard of that bar." Ben picked up his sandwich. "Supposed to be haunted, right?"

"Yes." Sarah laughed. "That's why Josie renamed it the Spirits and Spurs. Some claim my late father-in-law is one of the ghosts who makes an appearance from time to time. He used to stop in for a beer whenever Nelsie went into town to shop."

"Archie's supposed to be one of the ghosts?" This

was the first Molly had heard of it. "That needs to go into my notes. I have this feeling I'm missing all kinds of things that will just come out in casual conversation if I hang around long enough."

"That's true." Sarah sent her a fond glance. "You need to come back. You have summers off, right?"

"Sort of. I usually teach one session of summer school." She felt Ben's gaze on her. If she returned this summer, they could pick up where they left off. He'd be in Sheridan, which wasn't that far away, and in summer the drive would be easy. They wouldn't have to say goodbye forever.

"Then think about flying back up here," Pete said. "We've loved having you. You fit right in."

"Thank you. That sounds great." But she wasn't so sure it was a good idea. This time with Ben was short and sweet. When they parted, they'd make a clean break. If she came back, though, the relationship automatically became more complicated.

"Good." Pete seemed satisfied the issue was settled. He turned back to Ben. "You'll need to figure out where you're going to put these horses. Do you have some ideas about that?"

As the meal continued, Ben described his plans for buying a small spread on the outskirts of Sheridan, and Pete offered enthusiastic advice. The two of them seemed to have bonded. Nick and Gabe joined them, and soon the four men were deeply involved in a subject they all held dear.

Sarah glanced over at Molly and lowered her voice. "Are you okay?"

"I'm fine." She smiled to add emphasis to the statement.

Sarah leaned closer. "I hope you didn't have a disagreement with Ben."

"Heavens, no." Molly tried to control the heat in her cheeks but knew it was no use.

"You did, didn't you?" Sarah spoke in an undertone. "I thought you were getting along great last night, but you've avoided each other all morning. Was he rude to you?"

"No, Aunt Sarah. Everything's fine."

"Because I don't care if Pete likes him. If he's not nice to you, then he can take a long walk off a short—"

"Really, it's *fine*."

Sarah turned in her chair and skewered Molly with a look. "You're sure about that?"

Molly gulped. "Yes."

"All right." Sarah leaned even closer. "But since he's right down the hall from you, if there's any reason for concern, you let me know immediately. Is that clear?"

"Yes." But as she looked into Sarah's blue eyes, Molly didn't kid herself that she was fooling her aunt. Sarah knew that something was going on. She just didn't know for sure what it was.

But with the big party only three hours away, now was not the time to confess everything. No one had discovered the liaison with Ben yet.

Sarah nodded. "Good. Glad that's settled." She resumed her normal tone of voice. "I'm worried that we don't have enough wineglasses for tonight. We've lost more to breakage than I thought. I'm thinking of ditching the stemmed glasses completely and going with whiskey glasses for the wine. We have a ton of those. What do you think?"

"I think it's very European." Over Sarah's shoulder,

Molly caught Ben looking straight at her. One of the hands had come by to talk with Pete, temporarily interrupting the men's conversation.

Ben took the opportunity to wink at her. Then the ranch hand left and Ben returned to the topic of breeding horses. But that wink had undone her. He'd chosen the perfect moment to send her a covert message, a secret communication to remind her of their connection.

Molly had been looking forward to Sarah's party ever since she'd made plane reservations. She'd created a special photo album of all the Gallagher relatives, and each of them had written a birthday greeting next to their picture. Molly could hardly wait to present that to her aunt tonight, and now she was eager to see Sarah's reaction to the magnificent saddle.

And yet, her thoughts had already moved beyond the party to the moment when the guests had left and she could climb the stairs. She pictured slipping into her room and taking off her clothes. Unfortunately her bathrobe was fleece and had moose pictures on it, but that couldn't be helped.

"I just don't want the kids to think that the wine is their favorite cherry drink and guzzle it by mistake. I sometimes let them have the cherry drink in a whiskey glass, so help me keep an eye on them, okay?"

"I will." Molly did her best to concentrate on the conversation. "One sip and they'll spit it out. I've never known a kid who thought wine tasted good."

"Oh, I know one. Sarah Bianca took my glass when I wasn't looking the other night. When I asked if she'd tasted my wine, she assured me that she had, but it was okay because we had the same germs."

Molly laughed. "Sounds like her."

"So then I asked her opinion of the wine. She said it was yummy. I explained that it was for grownups, but I'm not convinced that she won't try it again."

"Then I'll keep close track of her." Sarah Bianca, SB for short, was Morgan and Gabe's oldest. During the cookie decorating session, the little redhead had informed Molly that she was not four, but four and a *half*, thank you very much. She thought her Grandma Sarah had hung the moon, and if her beloved grandmother loved red wine, so would SB.

Nick and Gabe said their goodbyes and left the table. Soon afterward, Pete and Ben pushed back their chairs and Pete glanced at his wife. "Unless you need me for something, Ben and I thought we'd head down to the barn and take another look at Calamity Sam, maybe turn him out so Ben can see him run."

"I think we're in pretty good shape." Sarah smiled at him. "I have a few more things to check on in the kitchen, but as far as I'm concerned, the work's done. We're ready for the party."

"Excellent." He leaned over and gave her a quick kiss on the cheek. "See you soon."

"Bye." Sarah gazed after the two men as they left the dining room. "You know, when Pete and Jack first told me a horse buyer was coming, I was so wrapped up in the preparations for the party and Christmas that I didn't think much about it." She turned back to Molly. "But don't you think his timing is a bit strange?"

"I guess it worked with his schedule." Molly hoped her expression gave nothing away.

Sarah gazed at her with a knowing smile. "That's BS."

"It is?"

"It is, and you know it. There's a secret connected to that guy. There has to be, and it has something to do with my birthday. I just hope it's not a horse. I love Bertha Mae and I don't need another one. But I don't think that's it. He didn't haul a horse trailer in here, just his pickup with a camper shell on the back."

Molly laid a hand on her arm. "My advice is to stop thinking about it."

"Oh, I intend to. But I had to test you and see if you were in on it, whatever it is. You definitely know what's going on. Maybe that's why you've been avoiding Ben all morning. You're afraid to talk to him for fear you'll give something away. Is that it? Did I guess?"

"I'll plead the Fifth."

Laughing, Sarah glanced out the window. "Sun's shining. If you want to take a walk, you could touch base with my husband and Ben and plot some more. I'll be in the kitchen with Mary Lou so I won't be able to hear a word you say."

"So you really aren't going to pry into this?"

"Nope. That would spoil the fun. I know better than to do that with this family. They do love their surprises."

"Then maybe I will walk down there." She thought it would be safe enough, even if temptation lurked in the form of Ben Radcliffe. He'd be with Pete, and ranch hands would likely be around, too. "I haven't spent much time at the barn. According to Nelsie's diary, she and Archie and my Grandpa Seth lived in it for a few months."

"Yes, they did. They were hardy, those two. I wish I could loan you her diaries to take home for your research, but I don't dare let them out of this house. The boys would kill me."

"I wouldn't dream of borrowing them, either. They're too precious. I feel lucky that I was able to read them, and I took copious notes and a few pictures of certain entries with my phone."

"The one where she mentioned you, I'll bet."

"Absolutely. I texted that one to my folks because I knew they'd get a kick out of it. I kind of remember her, but not very well. I was pretty young when she and Archie made their last trip to Arizona."

"That's too bad, because you would have loved her. I did." Sarah got a faraway look in her eyes. "When I first met her, she was younger than I am now. Hard to believe." She shook her head and scooted back her chair. "Enough of that. Go take your walk and don't let on that I suspect a thing."

"I won't."

"It doesn't matter if I do, anyway, since I have no idea what they could possibly be up to." She stood. "I have everything in the world a woman could want."

Molly stood, too. "Just remember that they love you and want you to know it."

"Oh, I do know it." She smiled. "They demonstrate how much they love me all the time and I return the favor. Life's too short to live any other way, don't you think?"

"Yes." Molly gave her a hug. "Thanks for letting me be a part of things for a few days, Aunt Sarah. I've thoroughly enjoyed it."

"You're more than welcome. Now, go put on your coat and get some fresh air. We might not get to keep this weather much longer. I heard there's a storm moving this way."

"See you in a few hours." Molly left the dining room and hurried upstairs. First she popped in her contacts. She probably wouldn't get to kiss Ben behind the barn, but she didn't know that for sure.

Then she put on her winter gear. She'd given the mittens their outing and was back to her leather gloves. She checked the weather app on her phone. Sarah was right about the approaching storm. With luck, the storm would blow through before Monday, when her plane left.

She had confidence it would. And Christmas Eve wasn't until Wednesday. Surely the storm, if it hit, would be over in time for her to spend the holiday with her family. She didn't intend to break a perfect record.

Dressed for winter, she bounded down the stairs and out through the front door. Someone had scraped the snow and ice from the porch, and the steps were clear, too. Sunlight glinted off the snow. She pulled on her gloves and shaded her eyes as she glanced toward the barn.

Ben and Pete stood by the fence watching Calamity Sam romp through the drifts in the pasture. The air was still cold enough that she could see her breath, but the sun helped warm her as she followed the path toward the barn.

A Paint horse running through snow proved to be a dramatic sight. As he frolicked, the white part of his coat blended into the background. If she squinted, she could almost see disembodied gray spots dancing in the air.

Mesmerizing though that was, Molly was more interested in studying Ben. She could get away with it because he had his back to her. The tilt of his Stetson, the sheepskin coat stretched across his broad shoulders and the booted foot he'd propped on the bottom rail of the fence all branded him as a cowboy, even though she'd never seen him ride. He made Western saddles and was thinking of buying one of the Last Chance horses. She figured he could ride.

She easily pictured him investing in a small ranch and adding a little horse breeding to his saddle-making operation. Like her, he was full of energy and ideas. He seemed to love life as much as she did. But she couldn't help thinking about his decision not to have children. If she and Ben were only destined for a brief affair, it shouldn't matter to her if he liked kids. She had no right to question his choices, either. Their relationship was based on sex, and she'd told him she was fine with that.

Except she wasn't. He'd already become more than a sex partner. His good nature and cheerful willingness to help out with the party preparations had impressed her. She was beginning to care about him and hated to think he was closing himself off from certain aspects of life out of fear.

His tenderness with her indicated he was a kind man, and she found it hard to believe that he'd mistreat a child. She also hadn't forgotten the emotion he'd put into his harmonica rendition of the theme from *Beauty and the Beast*.

Then there was his artistic side. He wouldn't have been able to create that magnificent saddle unless he had an empathetic, sensitive nature. His contradictions fascinated her. She wanted to know what made him

tick and why he nurtured some dreams while rejecting others.

He'd said that he'd come from an unhappy home and
didn't want to repeat the pattern. Tonight she'd watch
how he acted with Sarah's grandchildren. If he was
abrupt with them, she'd know that his concern was le-
gitimate and he was right not to want kids.

As she stood there contemplating this puzzle of a
man, he turned, along with Pete, and walked toward
her.

Pete called out a greeting. "Coming out to see Calamity Sam strut his stuff?"

"Sort of. Mostly I just craved a little fresh air."

As she drew closer, Pete lowered his voice. "Ben
said you know about the surprise."

"I do. The woman I called in Sheridan mentioned
that Ben made saddles, and I knew that had to be the
reason he was here."

Pete gazed at her. "Do you think Sarah has
guessed?"

"No."

"That's a relief. Ben and I mostly came out here to
discuss how to get the saddle into the house without
her noticing."

"Did you figure it out?" She had wondered about
the logistics.

"I think so. I'll keep Sarah busy in the bedroom
while…wait, that didn't come out right."

Molly grinned. "Whatever it takes, Uncle Pete."

He looked a little flustered. "What I meant to say
was that I'll distract her and keep her out of the living
room for the ten minutes it'll take for a couple of guys
to carry the stand and saddle into the house."

"We moved it to the front of the tractor barn first thing after we left the dining room," Ben said.

"And I finally got to see it," Pete said. "I was blown away. I've seen some gorgeous saddles, but this one… you made something very special, Ben."

He flushed. "Thanks."

"As long as Molly's out here, you should take her over to get a look."

Ben looked at her, his expression carefully neutral. "Would you like to do that?"

She smiled, enjoying the fact that they had their own special secret. "Of course!"

"You have never seen such a beautiful saddle in your life, Molly. Anyway, I need to get back. I forgot to check the supply of Scotch in the liquor cabinet. Usually I'm the only one who drinks that, but lately Alex has taken a liking to it."

Then he turned to Ben. "My apologies. I shouldn't throw out names like that. You'll need a scorecard to keep everyone straight tonight, but for the record, Alex Keller is Jack's brother-in-law. He and Jack's wife Josie are brother and sister."

"And Alex is married to Tyler, who is Morgan's sister," Molly added.

"Exactly." Pete nodded. "Stick close to Molly, Ben. She's been studying this stuff all week and she has it down cold."

"I'll be sure to do that." Ben's tone was carefully nonchalant.

"See you two later, then." Pete's long strides carried him back toward the house.

Ben glanced at her, laughter dancing in his brown eyes. "So, Molly, would you like to see that saddle?"

"Yes, Ben, I would love to."

"After you." He gestured toward the narrow path leading to the tractor barn.

As she walked ahead of him, she wondered what sort of scenario was going through his mind and if it was as X-rated as the one going through hers.

11

BEN DECIDED HE must be living right. From the minute
he'd turned away from the fence to find Molly standing several yards behind him, he'd been trying to figure out how he could get her alone. Pete had handed
him the perfect excuse.

But he wasn't going to mess things up by saying
anything incriminating while they made their way to
the tractor barn. Noise carried in the crisp air, and
ranch hands were in the barn cleaning out stalls while
some of the horses exercised in the pasture. The tractor barn was empty as far as he knew, though.

They couldn't be noisy in there, either. The place
echoed like crazy and he figured that sound could possibly be heard in the horse barn. He didn't want anyone
showing up to investigate.

Once they reached the tractor barn, he opened the
door for her and she slipped inside. They couldn't stay
long. Her red coat was a beacon that could be glimpsed
for miles.

He followed her in and called out. "Anybody here?"
The echo came back to him. No response, though. He

turned back toward the door, but there was no locking mechanism on the inside.

"What are you doing?" She moved close, almost touching him.

He breathed in her scent and his body responded immediately. "I'm looking for something to wedge the doors shut."

She left his side to prowl around. "There's a small workbench over here with a few tools on it."

"Perfect." He located a couple of wrenches and jammed one under each of the double doors. "That's just in case."

The interior of the barn was dim, but her smile lit it up. "Anyone would think you had plans to do something secretive in here."

"Anyone would be right." Unbuttoning his coat as he walked, he closed the gap between them. "You put in your contacts. Anyone would think you were hoping something like this might happen."

She laughed breathlessly. "Anyone would be right."

"We can't stay long, so we have to make every second count. Unzip your coat."

She pulled off her gloves first and tucked them into her pockets. Then she glanced around as she unzipped the puffy coat. "I don't see much in the way of a welcoming spot."

He chuckled. "Except you." He grabbed her around the waist and lifted her to the back fender of the first tractor in the row.

"Ben!"

"Shh. This place is an echo chamber. No matter what happens, don't yell, okay?"

"That could be a challenge."

"You're up to it." He pulled off one of her boots. "Unzip your jeans." He did the same.

"You seem to have this all worked out."

"I do." He freed his cock, which was ready for action. "My brain's been focused on the problem ever since Pete suggested I bring you in here to look at the saddle."

"Apparently other parts of you are focused on it, too."

He glanced up and discovered she was ogling his equipment. "I've had this problem all day long. You just didn't know about it." He took off his coat.

"You've been aroused all day?"

"Yep. Every time I looked at you I wanted to drag you into a dark corner and have my way with you." Reaching around her, he spread his coat on the fender, lining side up. "That's how you affect me."

"That's very flattering."

"That's very tough on my package. Now hang on to my shoulders, wrap your legs around my waist, and lift your cute little tush." When she did, he slid the coat under it.

"I have a feeling you've done this maneuver before."

"Never in a very cold tractor barn."

"Then maybe you shouldn't have taken off your coat."

"I plan to be plenty warm in a minute, and you need it." He set her back down so he could pull off her jeans and panties and work one of her legs completely free.

Her breathing sped up as she positioned herself on his coat, wiggling her bare fanny against it. "Kinky."

"Sorry. You're not staying there. Hang on to me." His heart was pounding by the time he slid both hands under her bottom and lifted her off the fender. "Wrap your legs around me again."

Once she did that, he found her entrance with the tip of his cock and let gravity take care of the rest.

"Mmm." She closed her eyes.

"I know." He tightened his jaw against a groan of pleasure.

She opened her eyes and excitement gleamed there. "I feel so decadent."

"Good. That should make it all the better." He sucked in air as she squeezed his cock hard. "Easy."

"You said we had to do this fast."

"Yeah." His grin was tight. "But we should have a little bit of fun, first. I'll lift you up and then you push yourself back down. I have a firm grip on you. You won't fall."

"I know I won't. I trust you."

"But you *will* come."

She held his gaze. "I know that, too."

"You have to be quiet, though."

She nodded. "You're still wearing your hat."

"No good place to put it. You're still wearing yours, too." He smiled. "I kind of like having sex with a woman wearing a red knit hat. I've never done that before."

"And I kind of like having sex with a man wearing a Stetson. I've never done that before, either."

"Then here we go." He eased her upward and she used the leverage gained from his shoulders to push back down. Dear God. He kept thinking that sex with her couldn't be as good as he imagined, but then he'd bury himself in her again and realize that, yes, it was just that good.

They established a tempo, one that slowly picked up as if by mutual consent. He watched her eyes darken and her lips part. Neither of them groaned or whimpered.

Even their breathing, though it was rapid, seemed softer. Without words or moans filling the silence surrounding them, the rhythmic beat of his thrusting became the dominant sound. The quicker the beat, the more he throbbed with anticipation.

Sweat trickled down his spine as he pumped faster. "Soon," he murmured.

She gulped. "Yes." Her fingers dug into his shoulders. A tremor moved through her.

"Come for me." He squeezed her smooth bottom as he pushed her upward one last time.

She shoved down again and he gasped as heat and motion swirled over his cock.

He watched her climax reflected in her eyes. Dragging in a breath, he surged upward and claimed his own climax. Holding her steady as he pulsed deep inside her took all the strength he had. If she'd weighed an ounce more, he wouldn't have been able to do it. She was perfect…so perfect.

When he began to shake, she smiled gently. "You need to put me down."

He nodded, but he didn't want to let her go. Easing away from her felt wrong. He wanted to carry her to the back of the tractor barn and find somewhere they could lie down and rest. Then they'd do it all again.

Instead, he tucked his still-twitching cock back inside his briefs and zipped up. Then he pulled a bandana out of his pocket and handed it to her so she could clean up. She kept it.

He didn't know if she planned to wash it and return it or keep it as a souvenir. Either way worked for him. He helped her back into her jeans and slid her boot on.

Once she was standing, he retrieved his coat and brushed the dust from the part that had come in contact with the tractor fender. The lining carried the subtle odor of sex, and that was fine with him, too. He put the coat on and breathed deep.

Then he laid his hat on the newly dusted fender and gathered her into his arms for one long, lazy kiss. He didn't want to leave the tractor barn without paying attention to her wonderful mouth.

In a way, kissing her was more personal than having sex, although he couldn't explain why. All he knew was that kissing Molly felt like a special privilege she'd granted him and he loved it. She responded with her signature enthusiasm. Apparently she enjoyed kissing him, too. Good to know.

With great reluctance he finally pulled back. "We need to go."

"I'm sure we do." She gazed up at him, her expression dreamy. "Your saddle is beautiful, but I doubt anyone would believe I spent this much time admiring it."

"Let's hope no one was clocking us." He stepped back but kept hold of both her hands. "I have such an urge to throw you over my shoulder and carry you off to…I don't know. Somewhere with a soft surface."

"I have such an urge to let you do that."

"But this party is important for both of us. You flew here so you could help your aunt celebrate, and I'm pretty excited about how she'll react to that saddle."

"She'll love it, but we'd better get moving, cowboy."

"Yeah." Squeezing her hands, he released her and picked up his hat.

"I'll get the wrenches." She pulled them out from under each door and handed them to him.

He put them back exactly where they'd been. Then he walked over to the doors. Just his luck, Jack's red truck pulled up in front of the tractor barn. Ben swore softly under his breath and closed the door.

"What's wrong?"

"Jack just drove up."

"So what? You brought me to the barn for a quick look at the saddle. He doesn't know how long we've been in here."

"No, but…" He surveyed her from head to toe. "You look well-kissed and extremely satisfied."

"You just think that because you know what we've been doing."

"I think that because it's true. And your hat's on crooked."

She straightened it. "Better?"

"A little. You still look…ah, never mind." One truck door slammed followed by a second. "Sounds as if Jack's bringing someone with him."

Ben walked over to where the saddle was perched on its stand and whipped the blanket off right before the door opened. He turned with a smile of welcome as Jack came in with a woman who wore her blond hair in a long braid down her back. Probably Josie. "Hey, Jack! Heard you drive up. Pete said there was some trouble with the plumbing at Spirits and Spurs."

"There was, but it's handled. Josie, this is Ben Radcliffe. Ben, my wife, Josie." Jack's tone was casual, but his gaze wasn't as he glanced from Ben to Molly.

"Pleased to meet you, Josie." Ben focused on her and tried to ignore the fact that Jack was sizing up the situation.

"Same here, Ben." Josie looked over at Molly. "Guess you couldn't stand the suspense either, huh?"

"Nope." Molly smiled. "And it's a beauty."

Ben still thought she looked like the cat that ate the canary. Intuition told him Jack was picking up on it. Could be trouble ahead.

Josie was protected from the cold like everyone else, in a bulky parka and a blue knit cap much like Molly's red one. Fortunately she was there to see the saddle, and it seemed to absorb all her attention. "Oh, my." She moved toward it and caressed the leather. "I'm no expert on saddles, but I've never seen one this pretty. Love the turquoise and silver accents."

"It's designed to fit Bertha Mae perfectly," Jack said. "We haven't tested that, but—"

"It'll fit," Ben said. "If it doesn't, I'll rebuild the saddle."

Josie's blue eyes widened as she turned to stare at him. "You'd start over?"

"If I have to. I stand by my work."

"I'm sure that won't be necessary," Jack said. "We provided Bertha Mae's measurements along with Mom's measurements to make sure that the saddle would be perfect."

Josie chuckled. "Sarah's measurements? How'd you get those, if you don't mind my asking?"

"Pete." Jack looked smug. "I didn't tell you about his scheme?"

"No, I missed hearing that story. I'm sure I'd have remembered."

"Pete's a sneaky guy. He bought her a one-of-a-kind outfit in Jackson that he knew for sure was too big. When she had to have it altered, he got all the specs from the seamstress."

"Goodness." Josie shook her head. "FYI, if you ever decide to give me a beautiful saddle like this, just ask me for my measurements instead of going through all that rigmarole. I'll be happy to give them to you."

Jack tipped his hat back with his thumb. "No need. I know your measurements."

"You most certainly do not! I'd bet there's no husband on the planet who knows his wife's measurements exactly."

"Test me sometime." Jack grinned at her.

"I will, and you'll be way off. Anyway, I love this saddle, Ben."

"I'm glad."

"Sarah will, too," Josie continued. "Don't you think so, Molly?"

"I do. Ben's done a wonderful job."

"Thanks, Molly." He knew she would have said that no matter what, and she'd told him last night the work was good, but hearing her say it again warmed him. He had come to value her opinion quite a bit.

He was in the awkward position of wanting her to think well of him, yet knowing in his heart he didn't deserve her good opinion. She trusted him when he didn't even trust himself. For the short time they'd be together, he could keep his flaws hidden, though. That was the advantage of knowing she'd leave on Monday. He wouldn't think about the sunshine that would leave with her.

"I texted Pete before we left Spirits and Spurs," Jack

said. "He seems to think we can risk moving the saddle up to the side of the house so it won't take so long to bring in after the party starts. I told him Josie and I would do that, but since you're here, Ben, you and I can carry it."

"Sure." Now that the unveiling was less than two hours away, Ben's chest tightened with anxiety. Everyone had praised the saddle, but Sarah was the one who had to be pleased. He'd know the minute she saw it whether she was or not.

"I think you should text him again and make sure Sarah's otherwise occupied," Josie said. "After all this, we don't want her to glance out the window and see you and Ben carrying something from the tractor barn. I don't care if it is covered with a blanket. She'll know what it is."

"Yeah, I'd better do that." Jack nudged back his hat and pulled out his cell phone. "Never would have believed I'd depend on this silly thing the way I do. I carry it everywhere now. Phone calls are bad enough, but texting is unmanly."

Josie held out her hand. "Want me to text Pete and protect your manhood, cowboy?"

"No." Jack scowled and moved his thumbs over the keyboard. "I'm just sayin'."

"Personally, I love that you carry your phone everywhere." Josie stuck her hands in her pockets. "Then you can't perform your manly disappearing act when there's an unpleasant chore to be done."

"My point, exactly." Jack glanced up from the phone. "Go ahead and cover the saddle, Ben. I'm sure we'll be hauling it out of here in a couple of minutes."

His phone chimed and he read the text. "Yep. Mom's taking a shower, so we're good to go."

Ben settled the blanket back over the saddle. The next time it was pulled off, he wouldn't be the one doing it. Something he'd labored over every day for two months was about to leave his care. That always felt strange. He had a picture of it on his phone, but he might never touch it again. He always felt a little sad when he had to part with one of his creations, and he'd put more of himself into this one than any other.

Jack tucked his phone into his jacket pocket. "Ladies, if you'll hold the doors for us, the manly men will carry this precious cargo out of here and over to the house."

Ben got on the front and Jack took the back, which was the same way they'd carried the saddle and stand into the barn. So much had happened since then.

"I'll back down the path," Jack said. "I know it better than you do."

"Okay." Maneuvering carefully, he guided the saddle through the door and let Jack set the pace. Molly and Josie followed. Judging from the bits of conversation Ben caught, they were talking about Molly's genealogy project.

"What's between you and Molly?" Jack's quiet question was abrupt, but not unexpected.

Ben met his gaze. "We like each other."

"Thought so. And I just realized I know almost nothing about you." Jack's breath fogged the air between them. "Careless of me."

"What do you want to know?"

"Are you unattached?"

"Yes."

"Where's your family?"

"Colorado."

"Visit them much?"

"No."

Jack frowned as if not happy with that answer. "Why not?"

"We…don't see eye to eye."

"Does Molly know about that?"

Ben hesitated. "I've mentioned it."

"Did you give her the details?"

"No."

"Then I suggest you do that." Jack's dark gaze hardened. "I suggest it very strongly. It's important information for a woman like Molly."

"You're right." Ben's gut clenched. He'd told himself Molly was better off not knowing the gritty details of his past. But she was an open book, so the scales weren't balanced when it came to their relationship. And they had one. He could no longer pretend otherwise. She might be coming back to Wyoming this summer. What then?

Yeah, it was time to give her the whole story. She deserved to know that she was dealing with a man terrified of losing his temper, afraid of who he'd become.

"And Ben?"

"Yeah?"

"If you don't treat her like the extremely valuable person she is, you'll answer to me. And it won't be pretty."

"Understood."

"You're one hell of a saddlemaker and I love what you've made for my mother, but hurt one of my own, and you'll wish we'd never met."

"I won't hurt her. You have my word."

Jack's smile was colder than the breeze sweeping down from the snow-covered mountains. "Break your word, Radcliffe, and I'll have your ass."

12

MOLLY HEARD JACK and Ben talking about something, but they spoke in low tones, as if they didn't want her or Josie to hear them. A couple of times Jack glanced in her direction. She couldn't shake the feeling they were discussing her. If so, then Jack suspected something.

Josie might, too, but Molly hadn't spent as much time with her as she had with Jack. Josie might not feel comfortable asking about Ben. Jack, on the other hand, allowed nothing to stand in the way of protecting those in his care. Sarah had told her that the other day, and now she'd seen it in action. When Jack had stepped into the tractor barn and spied her there with Ben, his whole manner had changed.

Sure, he continued to joke with his wife, but underneath that banter something in his tone made her think he was mentally arming himself to confront a potential threat. She appreciated the impulse, but she didn't want Jack to protect her from Ben. He reminded her so much of her brothers, who'd been intimidating her boyfriends ever since she'd turned sixteen and had been allowed, with major restrictions, to date.

Extreme protectiveness, both from her brothers and her parents, had been one of her reasons for moving into town instead of continuing to live at the family ranch. She was the only girl, which meant she'd had to fight for her sexual freedom. If she hadn't moved out, she'd probably still be a virgin.

No doubt her brothers would disapprove of her relationship with Ben, but they weren't here. Unfortunately, Jack was filling their role to perfection. She'd have to politely ask him to butt out, but finding a private moment to do that might be tough.

Right after Jack and Ben hid the saddle under a large tarp at the far end of the house, Jack slung an arm around Josie's shoulders. "Come on, babe. We need to shower and change for this shindig." They both hurried back to Jack's big red truck and drove away.

The wind had picked up, so Molly helped Ben tuck the canvas tarp more securely under the stand so it wouldn't flap. Maybe she was being paranoid about Jack's conversation with Ben. She should ask Ben about it before accusing Jack of meddling in her business.

Ben beat her to the punch. "Molly, we need to talk." He straightened. "Maybe out here's as good a place as any."

"Was I just the topic of conversation between you and Jack?"

"Yes, and—"

"Is he trying to protect me from you?"

"In a way, but that's not the point."

"It is the point. I'll speak with him. I'll let him know that this was mostly my idea. I don't want him to get the wrong impression of you. After all, you're hoping to do more business with him. I don't want to interfere in any way with that."

"That's fine, but I still—"

"Hey, are you Radcliffe?" A middle-aged ranch hand with a handlebar mustache walked toward them, his boots crunching through the snow drifts.

"I am."

"I'm Watkins." The man shook hands with Ben. "Glad I caught you. Hey, Molly."

"Hey, Watkins." Aunt Sarah had filled her in on the stocky cowboy's background. Two years ago, after a long courtship, Watkins had won Mary Lou's hand in marriage. Watkins had a first name, but nobody remembered what it was. He was also one of the guitar players scheduled to perform for tonight's party.

"Is the saddle under there?" Watkins peered at the tarp.

"Yep," Ben said, "but we'd better not uncover it again. I think we've finally got the blanket tucked around it good and tight."

"That's okay. I can wait until the party. I'm not here about the saddle." He was a good ten inches shorter than Ben and had to push back his hat and lift his chin to make eye contact. "I heard you might be willing to play a little harmonica with Trey and me tonight."

"I'd like that, if I wouldn't be in the way."

"Hell, no, son. We're not that slick. We'd love to have you, and I thought you might want to come on out to the barn. Trey's already down there with some of our music and our guitars. If you'll go fetch your harmonica, we can have a private jam session before the party and see what tunes we have in common."

"You bet. I'll be there in five minutes."

"See you then." Watkins headed for the barn.

Ben gazed at Molly. "What I have to say shouldn't be rushed, and I'd better go. I said I'd play tonight, so I don't want to duck out of it."

"You shouldn't. It'll be fun."

"But we'll have to talk later."

"Are you thinking of changing the plan?"

His hesitation gave her the answer.

"Maybe I shouldn't come to your room tonight. Jack must have put pressure on you to leave me alone." And she'd deal with Jack, but she might not be able to sway him. She'd also discovered he was stubborn. "I don't want to jeopardize—"

"Please come to my room tonight. But before we… before we do anything, I have some things to say."

"You have a crazy wife tucked away in an asylum?"

"No." His smile was sad. "Nothing that dramatic. Ready to go in?"

"Sure." They walked around the house and up the porch steps without speaking.

Once they were inside, Ben turned to her. "See you tonight." Then he bounded up the stairs to get his harmonica.

She debated whether to go up to her room and start getting ready. Normally she wouldn't need an hour to primp, but tonight was special. She wanted to wash her hair and spend time on her makeup. An hour might not even be enough.

Ben was coming back down as she pulled off her hat and started up the stairs. She gave him a quick smile. "Have fun."

"Thanks." His return smile was polite and brief.

With a sigh, she continued to her room. Too bad

her situation with Ben had come to a head this soon, but the family would have discovered their relationship eventually, maybe even during the party tonight.

Jack's reaction wasn't all that unusual, now that she had time to think about it. She was his youngest cousin from Arizona, and he'd never had sisters. That could make him even worse than her brothers when it came to interfering in her social life.

His concern was sweet, and she didn't want to be rude since she was a guest at this ranch. Although he wasn't the only one in charge, he had plenty to say about what went on here. On the surface, it looked as if Ben had taken advantage of Jack's hospitality by showing an interest in her.

Without giving offense or revealing how far the relationship had progressed, she wanted to convince Jack it was a two-way street. Ben shouldn't be blamed for something that she'd encouraged every step of the way. As Ben had said, they were both consenting adults and what they did in the privacy of his room was nobody else's business.

She didn't intend for anyone to know that she'd spent the night in his bed and hoped to spend tonight there, too. The layout of the huge house made it unlikely that anyone knew. If she was careful not to be seen entering or leaving his room, that part of their secret would be safe.

But Jack had planted a seed of doubt in Ben's mind. Clearly he was wondering if he should back off. The thought made her stomach twist. They might only have this brief time together, but she'd counted on making use of all of it.

If she were honest with herself, she'd have to admit

that she hoped this affair wouldn't end when she left Wyoming on Monday. Every moment she spent with Ben made him more precious to her. She didn't want to give him up at all, much less have their time shortened by Jack's influence.

If Ben's mind had changed, she'd just have to change it back. Fortunately, she had a killer dress in her closet. She'd brought it even though it might be a bit much for a family gathering. Jeans weren't right. She'd packed a more casual dress in case that had seemed more appropriate, but she was going for the wow factor tonight.

Thinking about the dress lifted her spirits. If her jeans and sweater turned Ben on, then this outfit would send him up in flames. If he had any thoughts of backing out of their agreement, she wanted him to know exactly what he was rejecting.

An hour later, she descended the stairs carefully, her wrapped gift in one hand, gripping the railing with the other. She looked hot, if she did say so herself. But her hotness quotient would be eliminated if she tripped in her four-inch heels and stumbled on the curved staircase. She also might damage the album she'd so carefully created for Aunt Sarah.

Laughter and the hum of conversation told her most of the guests had arrived. Her beauty routine had taken longer than usual, so she was about fifteen minutes late. The results, in her humble opinion, were well worth it.

She'd picked the knit dress off the rack because the moss green exactly matched her eyes. Then she'd tried it on, thinking that the long sleeves, ankle-length skirt and high neck would make it a fairly conservative choice. Oh, no. The dress slithered over her body like a second skin, leaving nothing to the imagination.

That alone would have made it sexy as hell, but the skirt was slit up one side to several inches above her knee. She hadn't noticed that, either, when she'd decided to try it on. Looking at herself in the dressing-room mirror, she'd seen a different Molly Gallagher, a seductive woman capable of driving men out of their minds. This was the dress's first outing, and after her wild night and stolen afternoon session with Ben, she felt qualified to wear it.

She'd bought teardrop earrings with stones the same color as the dress. She wore no other jewelry. The dress spoke for itself. Her hair was piled on top of her head and she had left a few tendrils dangling in front of her ears.

"Molly?"

She was halfway down the stairs when Ben called her name. She turned and looked over her shoulder. "Hi," she said. "You look nice." That was an understatement. He wore a crisp white Western shirt with silver piping that made his shoulders seem wider than ever, and his black dress jeans were sinfully snug.

His black leather belt was intricately tooled, and she wondered if he'd made it. He wore no hat tonight, and his thick hair gleamed in the light from the hallway. The scent of shampoo and shaving lotion drifted down the staircase. She had an almost irresistible urge to climb back up and kiss his smooth jaw. But judging from the heat in his brown eyes, she didn't dare.

"You look…" He swallowed. "I don't even know how to describe how you look, Molly. That dress really…it fits you like…I've never seen a dress look as good on anybody as that one does on you."

"Thank you." It was exactly the response she'd hoped for. She'd never felt more beautiful or desirable in her life.

"Hang on a minute. I'll walk down with you." He started toward her.

"Got your harmonica?"

He patted his breast pocket. "Right here. Watkins and Trey are good. I'll have to bring my A game tonight."

"From what I heard before, you'll be fine." She smiled at him.

He paused and caught his breath. "Damn, Molly. You're so…damn."

"What?" She pretended not to know what he meant. But she knew, and exulted in a sexual power she'd never claimed before.

"That dress. It moves when you move. It slides right over your breasts and your sweet little bottom. I don't—hell, I know it's unworthy of me, but I don't want other men to see how great you look."

"Too late." Jack stood at the bottom of the stairs with Josie. "Put your eyes back in your damned head, Radcliffe." He held out his hand. "Come on, Cousin Molly. Let's go join the party. You look terrific, by the way."

"Thank you." She walked down the stairs, took his hand and allowed him to steady her for the last few steps.

"That dress is dynamite," Josie said.

"Yours isn't too shabby, either." Molly admired the ice-blue, long-sleeved sheath that Josie had accented with silver shoes and jewelry. Instead of her usual braid, she'd created an updo that showed off her slender neck. She was a knockout.

Jack gave Josie a possessive once-over. "Not shabby at all," he said softly. "I'm a lucky man."

He crooked both arms. "Ladies, make me the envy of every poor slob in the room."

"I'm honored, Jack." Molly looked into eyes that glowed with the pride of his Shoshone ancestors. She might as well make her stand now as later. She knew instinctively that he'd respect her for being direct. "But I'm going to wait for Ben."

Jack's glance flicked from Molly to Ben, who'd remained standing midway down the staircase. "All right." He held Ben's gaze. "Don't forget our conversation."

Ben's voice was steady. "I won't."

Jack and Josie walked into the living room and Molly took a shaky breath. Round One. She thought maybe she'd won it, but time would tell.

"Thank you." Ben descended the last few steps and stood before her. "But you didn't have to do that."

"Yes, I did." She looked into his eyes. "I'm capable of choosing my own…friends. Jack needs to understand that."

A smile teased the corners of his mouth. "I'm glad you consider me a friend."

"I do." She longed to touch him. But while they were within sight of the front door where anyone could come in and discover them, being affectionate might not be the best plan. "You may not realize it, but you've given me enormous confidence."

"You?" He looked surprised. "You were already confident. You didn't need me for that."

"Ah, but you're wrong." She lowered her voice. "When you asked me to pirouette for you at the top of the stairs twenty-four hours ago, I wasn't completely convinced of my sexual power. Thanks to you, now I am." She stretched out her arms. "Behold the result."

He laughed, his eyes sparkling. "So as I struggle to make it through this evening of torture, watching you move through the crowd in that incredible dress, I have only myself to blame?"

"Pretty much."

"In a twisted kind of way, that helps. Shall we go in?"

"Yes." She linked her arm through his. "I can hardly wait to hear you play."

"Then know this. Every note will be for you."

His words ran in a continuous loop in her mind as they walked into the crowded living room. They were the kind of words that could turn a girl's head. If Ben were a different sort of man, she'd think he'd used them as a seductive line.

But he didn't need to spout pretty words to get a woman into bed. He'd already accomplished that with her. She'd spent enough time with him, especially quality time in which emotional barriers had come down, to know that he didn't say anything he didn't mean.

He'd announced from the beginning that he was the wrong man for her, long-term. She still didn't know all the particulars, but he hadn't tried to fool her by implying that they could have more than a brief fling. He'd been honest about that from the beginning.

Jack might not completely trust him, but she did. She really should corner Jack and discuss his dealings with Ben. Jack hadn't turned in his genealogy homework yet, and that would give her a good excuse to talk with him.

For right now, though, she was a party girl on the arm of a handsome man as they walked into a kaleidoscope of color and movement. As Molly deposited her wrapped package on the gift table, Ben went to get them both drinks. Before he made it to the temporary bar set up along the far wall, Watkins grabbed him and pulled him into the corner where Trey was setting up their sound system.

Molly hadn't thought about the fact that Ben would be needed over there. She'd never attended a function with someone who was part of the evening's entertainment. Making her way over, she tapped him on the shoulder.

He turned. "Oh, sorry. I'll get our drinks in a second. First I need to—"

"Never mind. You have things to do. Can I bring you something?"

He grinned. "One of those dark beers would be outstanding."

"Got it." She wove through the crowd, greeting those she'd already met, like Pam Mulholland, Nick's aunt and one of Sarah's best friends. Last Christmas Pam had married Emmett Sterling, the tall, sixty-something ranch foreman standing between her and his daughter Emily. Emily was in line to be foreman after Emmett retired.

Emily's husband, Clay Whitaker, director of the stud program at the ranch, arrived loaded down with two bottles of beer and two glasses of wine. "Hey, Molly. Can I get you something from the bar?"

"Thanks, but I promised Ben I'd fetch his drink, so

I need to go there, anyway. By the way, who's the couple standing by the Christmas tree talking to Jack?"

"They're good friends of Jack's," Clay said. "Nash and Bethany own the ranch that borders this one."

"And Bethany writes self-help books," Pam added.

"Right! I remember Aunt Sarah mentioning that."

"Except for the ranch hands, they might be the only ones who aren't somehow part of the extended family," Pam said. "But apparently Nash and Jack were inseparable in high school, so I think Sarah thinks of him as another son."

Molly glanced around at the crowd gathered in the living room. "Such a happy group."

"I know." Pam smiled. "It's a real tribute to Sarah that everyone's so eager to help her celebrate her big birthday."

"Yes, it is. I'm so glad I made the trip. Anyway, I did promise Ben that drink, so I'd better get going. I'll catch you all later!"

But she got sidetracked briefly when she stopped to talk to Regan O'Connelli and his fiancée, Lily King. Regan shared a veterinarian practice with Nick, and he was also Morgan and Tyler's brother. Lily ran an equine rescue operation on the outskirts of Shoshone.

Eventually Molly reached the bar. It was so tempting to stop and talk to people. Tonight was a genealogist's dream. She was finally able to put faces to some of the names on her chart.

A guy with a buzz cut was tending bar. She'd never seen him before, so she held out her hand. "Hi, I'm Molly, a cousin from Arizona."

He smiled and shook her hand. "I'm Steve, a bartender from Spirits and Spurs. I'm absolutely no relation to anybody here, which Josie thought would be a good thing so I can concentrate on the job at hand. What can I get for you?"

She asked for a glass of the red wine Sarah had introduced her to and a bottle of dark beer. Then she returned to the makeshift bandstand and handed the bottle to Ben.

"Thanks." He glanced toward the hallway that led to Pete and Sarah's bedroom. "Pete just coaxed her back there on some pretext or other. I think this is it."

She noticed his breathing had changed and lines of tension bracketed his mouth. "Nervous?"

"Hell, yes. What if she doesn't like it?"

"She'll love it. Everyone else has."

"I know, but they're not the ones I made it for." He looked over at the front door. "They're bringing it in." His voice was strained.

She'd never dreamed that he'd be so worried about whether Sarah would like the saddle. So far, everyone had raved about it, but he was right that Sarah's reaction was the crucial one. If she gave the slightest indication that she didn't love it, Ben would be cut to the quick.

His anxiety became hers, and she longed to hold his hand, touch his arm, anything that would let him know she was there for him, but he wouldn't appreciate that. She might know he was feeling vulnerable, but he wouldn't want anyone else to figure it out. Outwardly he projected calm confidence in his ability to do his work.

She'd never thought about the pressure on an artist when a creation was unveiled. Ben's work was more than just a job, and she wondered how many of his customers understood that. Now that she'd seen this saddle, she longed to visit his shop and ask more questions about the process. That wouldn't happen if they ended things when this interlude was over.

Gabe and Nick carried the still-covered saddle into the middle of the room and moved back as conversation hummed all around them. Jack called down the hall to Pete before walking back to stand beside the saddle. Everyone's attention shifted to the arrival of the birthday girl.

Pete held Sarah's hand as he ushered her into the living room. She'd chosen to wear winter white, a stunning dress that showcased her cherished turquoise jewelry. Her cheeks were pink with excitement.

Molly held her breath along with everyone else in the room. She desperately wanted Sarah to love the saddle for Ben's sake.

Then little Sarah Bianca, her evergreen dress decorated with ruffles and a tiara balanced on her red curls, jumped up and down with cries of glee. "Do it, do it, Uncle Jack!" she shouted. "Show Grandma her surprise!"

"Yeah, yeah!" Archie, her blond, three-year-old cousin, started jumping, too. "Do it, Daddy!"

With a smile, Jack stepped forward. "Happy birthday, Mom. From all of us." He whipped off the blanket.

Sarah stared at the saddle in complete astonishment. Then she began to cry.

Ben sucked in a breath. "Is that good?"

"Oh, yeah." Molly's eyes filled as she watched tears of joy flow down Sarah's cheeks. "She loves it."

"But she's *crying*."

Molly sniffed. "That's because she's happy, and

touched and overwhelmed by the generosity of everyone. The saddle's a hit, Ben. You did it."

"Thank God."

Sarah wiped her cheeks and accepted a handkerchief from Pete. She blew her nose and handed it back to him, which brought a laugh from the group and broke the tension. Everyone clapped and cheered as Sarah walked over to stroke the leather of the saddle and exclaim over the beauty of it.

Finally she looked up and searched the room until her gaze settled on Ben. "You made this, didn't you?"

"Yes, ma'am."

"It's magnificent."

"Thank you." His voice was husky.

"I knew you weren't here to buy a horse. But I never imagined…" She went back to stroking the leather with reverence. "I've never had a saddle like this. Bertha Mae will strut like a queen."

She lifted her head again and glanced around the room. "Thank you, all of you. It means more than I can say." Her voice caught, and she swallowed. "I can't imagine a better birthday gift than this, except to have you all here to share it with me."

More cheers followed. Then the grandchildren crowded around and asked to sit on the saddle. She lifted each one in turn, while camera phones clicked. Everyone laughed at the kids looking so proud sitting on their grandmother's birthday saddle.

Molly turned back to Ben. "Do you mind that the kids are sitting on it?"

"Why should I?" He watched with a smile.

"I don't know. It's a valuable saddle. Maybe you'd rather not see little kids bouncing on it."

"They can't hurt it. Obviously they're having fun, so why not?"

From the corner of her eye, she studied him. He didn't seem to be faking his enjoyment of the scene, which seemed odd for a man who'd decided not to have kids. The puzzle of Ben Radcliffe became more complicated than ever.

13

THE MUSIC STARTED after that, and Ben threw himself into the first set. He knew most of the tunes, and they were lively and easy to play. Because they didn't challenge him too much, he could watch Sarah with her grandchildren.

The saddle still sat in the middle of the room and dancers maneuvered around it. Sarah stood beside the saddle and rotated the kids on and off, giving each a turn, even Gabe's youngest, a months-old baby.

An older boy, who could be a teenager but looked younger because of his small size, climbed up and smiled at Nick. "What d'ya think, Dad?"

"I think you need to start saving your allowance, Lester," Nick said with a grin.

Such a simple exchange, and yet so filled with subtext. Lester had hinted he wanted a fancy saddle, and his father had good-naturedly told him he'd have to save for it. That's what a loving relationship between a father and son looked like. Ben had never experienced it.

He never would have dared to hint that he wanted

something. That would have been a sure way to get a lecture on his ungrateful behavior, or maybe even a beating. He'd learned early to keep his mouth shut and his head down.

The scene of Sarah with her family affected Ben in ways he hadn't anticipated. Unexpected yearning tightened his throat and at times made him screw up a note. He doubted anyone noticed, but it bothered him.

Then he'd catch a glimpse of Molly laughing with some of the women, or dancing with one of her Chance cousins, and he'd miss another note. Her joyful smile stirred longings he'd kept buried for years.

He didn't like feeling this way. He'd carefully avoided strong emotions for most of his life because he'd seen the dark side. When gripped by powerful emotions, people became unpredictable. The line between love and hate was thin and easily breached.

When he'd taken on this commission, he hadn't planned on having it throw him off kilter. He'd known that spending a couple of days at the Last Chance Ranch would be intellectually interesting, a scientific trip to observe a normal family. He'd planned to hold himself emotionally distant.

Molly had blown that plan all to hell on his first night here. He wanted her in a way he'd never wanted another woman, despite knowing he couldn't make her happy. She'd gotten under his skin. No, he'd *allowed* her to get under his skin. For some reason, he'd let down his guard and she'd stormed the castle.

That was bad enough, and he dreaded the conversation they would have tonight after the party. He was pretty sure she was fantasizing that they had a future, after all. She couldn't help it, optimist that she was, and he glimpsed dreams of forever shining in her green eyes. He'd have to destroy those dreams and watch the sunshine disappear.

Adding to that disaster, he was currently surrounded by the intense love that permeated the Chance family. He'd tried to maintain his position as an outsider, but Sarah had brought him right into the center of the celebration with her gratitude. With her tears. Her reaction had annihilated his defenses. He'd seen his mother cry in despair, but he'd never seen any woman cry with joy. His world had shifted.

He wanted this, all of it, but he didn't trust himself to create it. He could build a saddle, but he didn't know how to build a life. Not this kind of life where people hugged each other, watched out for each other, defended each other from any threat.

As Jack had. Ben didn't blame him one damn bit. Jack was right to worry about Ben getting too close to Molly. And he was too close to her. If he cared this much, then she probably cared more. Her heart was in shape for loving. His wasn't.

The set ended, and Sarah glanced up. Her gaze steady, she excused herself from a conversation with Josie and walked toward him. He braced himself.

"I don't know how to thank you." She placed a warm hand on his arm as she looked into his eyes. "It's obvious to me that you put all kinds of love into that saddle."

He hadn't known what to expect when she'd come over, but certainly not that. Damn it, his throat was tightening up again. He cleared it. "I enjoyed making it."

"I know you did. Jack said you made it in only two months. You must have burned the midnight oil."

"It was a pleasure." He kept thinking of how she'd cried when she'd first seen it. "I…I hoped it would be what you wanted."

"It's as if you knew what would suit me. I suppose Jack helped give you an idea of who I am, but you must have used your instincts, too."

"Maybe so." He didn't trust himself to say more without emotion roughening his voice.

"It's been wonderful having you as a guest, Ben. You're like a long-lost member of the family. I hope that's all right for me to say. From things you've said, I gather you're not…close…to your family."

He swallowed

"I just want you to know that you're welcome here anytime." She squeezed his arm. "Anytime at all." Then she gave him a little pat and walked away as if sensing that he wasn't in command of himself.

Tucking his harmonica into his shirt pocket, he walked out of the room and took the stairs two at a time before he did something embarrassing like break down. He had the urge to pack his things and leave, but the wind had begun to howl outside. The storm would hit any minute. He was a fool, but not that much of one.

So, instead, he sat on the edge of the bed, his head in his hands, while he struggled to breathe. In one precious moment, with a few words of praise, Sarah had warmed his heart in a way his own mother never had. His father had forbidden any gentleness for fear his boys would become sissies. His mother had never argued with that.

"Ben?"

He glanced up. Molly stood in the doorway. He

should have known she'd see him leave and follow him up here. That was Molly. Caring, compassionate, loving.

"What's wrong?"

He looked into those green eyes filled with concern. "Everything."

"How can that be?" She walked over and knelt at his feet as she placed her hands on his knees. "Aunt Sarah loves the saddle. I saw her come over and tell you again how much she loves it. I couldn't figure out why that made you take off like you did."

He cupped her sweet face in both hands. "That's because you come from a loving family where gestures like Sarah's happen all the time. But I...I can't handle it."

"Why?"

"I was raised with fear instead of love. My dad's anger was a terrifying thing to me and my older brother. He didn't hit us a lot, but the threat of it was always there. I don't know that he ever hit my mother, but he criticized her constantly. Still does. She has zero self-confidence."

"Oh, Ben." Moisture gathered in her eyes. "I was afraid that's what you'd hinted at before. I'm so sorry."

"Please don't cry." He heard the frantic note in his voice and hated it.

She blinked and her jaw firmed beneath his touch. "I won't. Tell me what you need."

"To be magically transported out of this house and back to a life I've learned how to handle."

"Sorry, that's beyond my powers."

He smiled as the tight band around his chest loosened. "And here I thought you could do anything."

"I'm awesome, but I can't teleport people. At least, not yet."

She was so good at this, he thought. So good at comforting people and putting them at ease. He'd even recovered enough to joke with her. "Sex is another good option, but we're not doing that, either."

"I'm afraid you're right. Sorry. Now is not the best time for wild monkey sex."

"Damn. Then I may just have to go back down there and act like everything is peachy." But thanks to her calming presence, he felt as if he could do that.

"Ben, I have to ask, although I think I know the answer. Is your family background why you don't want kids?"

"Yep, that's it." Saying it was easier than he'd thought it would be. "I hate the way my father ruled the household, and my brother swore he did, too, but he's exactly the same kind of father to his kids. And he intimidates his wife, who scrambles to please him."

"And you think you would turn out that way, too?"

He brushed his thumbs over her warm cheeks. "It's all I knew growing up, so I could easily slide right into that pattern. If I do marry someday, it would be with the understanding she should leave me the minute I start behaving like my father. But kids—they can't just leave."

"I know, but—"

"I'm not having kids, Molly. I won't risk repeating the cycle the way my brother has." He looked into her eyes. "Jack wanted me to make sure you understood all that. He said it was important information for a woman like you."

"A woman like me?" She bristled. "What's that supposed to mean?"

"Well..." He suspected he might get into trouble if he didn't choose his words carefully. "You come from a big, loving family, so logically, you probably want that for yourself."

"Yes, eventually! But *a woman like me* doesn't hand every guy I date a checklist to make sure he wants marriage and a big family, and the sooner the better!"

He shouldn't smile, but he couldn't help it. "You might want to tell Jack that. He probably thinks you do."

"Don't worry. I plan to have a talk with Cousin Jack."

"He's just afraid that you'll get hooked on me, and I'm not the right man for you."

"Jack's not in charge of my love life."

"I know."

"You told me right away that you weren't the right guy for me because you didn't want a family. Then I found out that you'd had a vasectomy. Now I have the whole story as to why. That doesn't mean I don't want to have sex with you anymore."

He searched her gaze. "Can you honestly say you've never thought that maybe, with time, we'd work something out between us?"

"Um..." Color darkened her cheeks.

"See?"

"Mostly after I saw the way you watched Sarah with her grandkids. I had wondered if you disliked children, but you don't."

"No. I like them a lot. That's why I can't take a chance on lousing up my own."

"You don't know that you would!"

"I don't know that I wouldn't. Listen, Molly, I made up my mind about this when I had the vasectomy."

"Sometimes those can be reversed."

"I don't want it reversed. I've read enough to know my dad has a borderline personality disorder. Maybe that's genetic. I didn't know my grandfather, but from the stories I've heard, he was the same way. Maybe that's just what he was taught, but maybe not."

"Then you could adopt."

He sighed. "I'd still be putting some innocent kid at risk. I can't take that chance."

"But—"

"Molly, the way you keep arguing the point, I have to wonder if you *are* thinking I'll change my mind about a relationship."

"That's bullshit." She scrambled to her feet and teetered as she regained her balance on her high heels. "And don't look so shocked. I know how to swear. I have brothers."

He closed his mouth, which had, in fact, dropped open when she let loose with that word. "Then you can probably outswear me. I only lived with one older brother."

She didn't smile. If anything, she looked angrier than ever. "As for your assumption about why I'm suggesting that you could find a way to have a family even with a vasectomy, has it occurred to you that I'm saying that for *your* sake?"

"My sake?"

"Yes, your sake. You should have seen the expression on your face while Sarah played with the kids on that saddle. You were eating it up with a spoon. Just try and tell me that you wouldn't like to have cute little kids like that running around, and eventually grand-kids, and a family gathering like this one. Because I know you would!"

"So what?" He stood, too. He wished she couldn't read him so well, but it was partly his own damned fault. He'd been more open about his feelings since he'd met her and that needed to stop. "Doesn't matter what I want. My brother went into his marriage bound and determined not to be like Dad. Now he's exactly like him. When I mention that, and I have, he yells at me and says I don't know what I'm talking about."

"That doesn't have to be you! Don't cut yourself off from life just because —"

"Stop it, Molly. They're starting up the music again. I need to get down there." He walked past her and out the door. It hurt like hell to be so abrupt with her. He'd probably hurt her, too.

But she didn't understand the terror he felt at the possibility he'd recreate his parents' lives, or his broth-er's. If she understood, she wouldn't keep arguing with him.

She might think she'd known what kind of man he was, but she hadn't, not really. Even when faced with the truth about him, she was trying to make bargains and change things so it would all come out roses and lollipops. Of course she was. That was Molly, a bun-dle of sunshine.

It was the quality that had drawn him to her. Appar-ently he'd thought he could use her light and warmth to ease the cold darkness in his soul. That had been so damned selfish of him.

When he walked back into the living room, he discovered the configuration had changed. The saddle had been moved next to the Christmas tree, which opened the entire space for dancing. A woman Ben hadn't met was harmonizing with Trey on the Tim McGraw and Faith Hill number "I Need You." And only two people were out on the floor. Pete and Sarah danced looking into each other's eyes as if, in this moment, no one else existed.

Ben stood at the edge of the room, his heart once again lodged in his throat.

"Beautiful, isn't it?" Molly appeared next to him and gazed at the couple circling the floor.

"Yes."

Her fingers slipped through his.

God help him, he tightened his fingers and held on, needing her more than he needed to breathe. Jack could take him out and shoot him at dawn, a fate he no doubt deserved. But if Molly couldn't be turned away by all that he'd said to her, if she was willing to hold his hand and give him comfort for the short time they were together, he would take it.

The dance ended with Pete giving Sarah a soft kiss. Then he grinned and beckoned to everyone surrounding the dance floor. "Show's over. Get out here and we'll all play bumper cars again."

"Come on." Molly tugged him forward. "Dance with me. My extra four inches should make it way easier. I won't have to stare at your belt buckle."

That made him smile. Molly didn't stay down for long. She might have been arguing with him five minutes ago, but she wasn't going to let that spoil her mood. "It's a great offer, but I should get back to Trey and Watkins."

"They can manage without you for one more song. It's a slow one, so you'll have plenty of breath left over to play your harmonica. Come on. You know you want to. You've been giving me cow eyes all night."

"Cow eyes? I don't *think* so." But he let her pull him out into the crowd. Once she was in his arms and his palm felt the slide of that green knit material against the small of her back, he was very glad she'd talked him into it.

"Cow eyes." She looked up at him. "Like this." Her expression changed to one of complete adoration.

He lost it. Maybe it was the tension he'd been under, but he started laughing so hard he could barely dance. He twirled her around and bumped into Jack and Josie. "Sorry. Brakes just went out."

Jack gave him a long-suffering look, but a smile twitched the corners of his mouth. Maybe Jack wasn't quite such a hard-ass after all. Ben hoped not, because he'd rather be the guy's friend than his sworn enemy. And that was disregarding the possibility of doing more business with him. Ben plain liked him. Admired him, in fact.

Jack had it figured out. He and Josie seemed to be on equal footing in a loving relationship. Just then, Sarah danced by with her grandson Archie in her arms. He looked overjoyed to be there. Apparently the kid was bright and well-adjusted, which was no surprise given his environment.

Molly snuggled closer and laid her head against his shoulder. Whereupon Ben forgot all about Jack and the rest of the Chance clan. Resting his cheek on her hair, he forgot everyone in the room except the woman in his arms.

If he had Molly in his life, maybe he could learn how to create what Jack had. For one shining moment he allowed himself to imagine what that could be like. But it would be a gamble, and a huge one at that. He'd be gambling with her life as well as his own.

He cared about her more than he'd cared about any woman he'd been with, maybe more than any person he knew. His shiny picture collapsed into a heap of dust. He simply couldn't ask her to take that risk. They'd have this interlude, and he'd make the most of it if she was willing. But then he'd get out of her life. It was for her own good.

14

MOLLY KNEW THERE was an excellent chance Ben would break her heart, especially after their dance. She'd admitted to herself that this was no longer a fling, and not just for her. He was way more invested than he'd ever confess.

But his psychological wounds ran deep. They had to, in order for him to undergo surgery so he wouldn't father any children. Not many men would take such a step, but ironically, it showed how much he cared about those children he would never have. He was protecting them before they even existed. What a selfless act.

He wouldn't see it that way, of course. And she wouldn't point it out to him, either. Instead, she'd drop the subject completely and savor whatever time they had together. If she hoped for a miracle, some epiphany that would allow him to see he would never be like his father or his brother, then that only made her human.

During the next break in the music, Sarah sat in one of the easy chairs pushed back against the wall and opened the rest of her presents, including Molly's album. Her face lit up as she turned the pages carefully, reading the birthday wishes written beside each picture.

Molly was thrilled with Sarah's reaction, but not surprised. Sarah was easy to predict. Ben, on the other hand, was not.

To her amazement, he stood beside her in the crowd gathered around Sarah and rested his hand on her shoulder. He no longer seemed worried about Jack's dire warnings, and when Sarah exclaimed over the album, he gave Molly's shoulder a quick, affectionate squeeze.

Once during the opening of the presents, she caught Jack giving Ben an assessing glance. But his expression wasn't nearly as fierce as it had been when he'd confronted Ben at the foot of the stairs. Maybe Jack had noticed the exchange between his mother and Ben, and had decided to give the newcomer the benefit of the doubt.

Food was served buffet style. Molly found a footstool to sit on, and Ben crouched next to her to share the meal.

"Jack seems to have mellowed," she said quietly.

"Yeah, I noticed that, too." He glanced at her. "Wouldn't have mattered if he had or not. You seem to be willing to take me as I am, so unless Jack orders me out of the house, I thought I'd stick around."

Warmth flooded through her. "Good."

"'Course, I might not have a whole lot of choice. The storm's kicking up pretty good out there. Sarah and Pete could have some unexpected overnight guests."

"I hadn't thought of that." She held his gaze. "If it's too dangerous for everyone to head home…"

"I'll be giving up my room and moving somewhere

else. I could sleep on the floor down here, if necessary, but I can't justify keeping a king-sized bed all
to myself."

"I suppose not." She took note of the snow hitting
the living room windows with more force.

"We'll roll with whatever happens. But I figure I'll
stay on until Monday, in any case, and drive you to the
airport. It's on my way and everyone will be involved
in Christmas stuff so it makes sense for me to do it."

She smiled. "I'd like that. Thank you."

"Consider it settled, then. And if we lose tonight,
we'll just have to make up for it tomorrow night."

"Make up for what?" Sarah Bianca showed up, her
green eyes focused on Ben.

"Sleep," Molly said immediately.

"I know." The little girl regarded them with a smug
expression. "I get to stay up really, really *late*. Mommy
says we might even sleep over. We do that sometimes
when it snows hard." She took a sip from her glass.

"That'll be fun," Molly said. "Whatcha got there?"

"My cherry drink."

Molly remembered her promise to keep an eye on
SB's choice of beverage. "Can I taste it?"

"Sure." Sarah Bianca held it out.

Molly took a quick sip and confirmed that it wasn't
wine. "Delicious." She handed the glass back.

"Grandma already tasted it. Then Uncle Jack wanted
to taste it, too! Everybody wants to taste my drink all
of a sudden." She looked at Ben. "Do you want to?"

"Thank you, but no. I have my beer."

"I don't like that beer. I tried Uncle Jack's once and
it was yucky. But I like Grandma's wine. She says I

can't have it until I'm waaaaay older, like *you*." She pointed a finger at Molly.

Ben's lips twitched as if fighting the urge to laugh. "She's right. Your Grandma's a smart lady."

"I know." She studied him with the solemn intensity of a four-year-old. "Did you really make that saddle?"

"Yes, I did."

"How?"

"Well, I start with a frame that's made of wood, and the frame has to fit the horse, in this case, Bertha Mae."

"Wood?" Her smooth forehead creased in a frown. "I didn't see any wood."

"That's because it's covered with leather. Stretching the leather over the wood is tricky. I never know if it'll work out the way I hope."

SB took a sip from her glass with the sophistication of a debutante. "Sometimes that happens to me when I make things."

Ben smiled. "It happens to me *all* the time. But I just keep working at it until I get it right."

"Me, too." She paused to take another drink. "Someday I'll make a saddle."

"Excellent." Ben nodded. "It's a challenge, but it's worth it."

"And I'll make it pretty, like you did. With stuff on it. And maybe even *ribbons*."

"That would be very interesting. I'd like to see that."

Molly's heart melted. He was a natural with kids. If only he'd give himself credit.

"When I make my saddle, I'll show you it. Well, I have to go. My mommy said I shouldn't stay over here too long."

"Oh?" Ben lifted his eyebrows. "Why not?"

"Because. She said you might want to be alone with *Molly*." She giggled and walked away.

Ben chuckled. "She's quite a kid."

"You were very good with her."

He gave her a long look. "It's easy when they're being cute. Anyone would do the same."

"Not necessarily." She knew she was on thin ice with this topic, but she desperately wanted him to see all the things he was doing right. "They might brush off her question about how they made the saddle. They might belittle her announcement that she was going to make one of her own someday. You didn't."

He gazed at her silently before taking a deep breath. "So I was nice to Sarah Bianca, the granddaughter of my hostess. I was taught to be polite. It proves nothing."

What a stubborn, damaged man. She longed to take him by the ears and force him to see reason, but she'd only drive him away. No one wanted to spend time with a person who was trying to fix him. "Guess not."

His expression gentled. "I know you mean well, Molly. Your belief in the goodness of others is one of the things that I'm drawn to."

She was drawn to the goodness in *him*, but if she said that he'd hear it as another attempt to influence his thinking.

"I'm sure I frustrate the hell out of you." He smiled. "I must seem like a man from a foreign country who doesn't quite understand your language. It's a wonder we get along as well as we do."

She didn't think it was a mystery. They were more alike than different, but he wasn't willing to see that. Maybe he never would. He certainly never would if she pestered him about it.

"But we do get along." She looked into his eyes. "Especially in one particular area."

His breath caught. Then he lowered his voice. "Then we still have a date after this party is over?"

"Assuming everyone goes home and you're not too tired."

"You're kidding, right?"

"Not really. Your mouth has gotten quite a work-out on that harmonica. You might want to rest it."

"That's how much you know." He grinned. "Playing the harmonica just warms up my mouth for…other things." He waggled his eyebrows.

She sucked in a breath as her blood heated.

"Careful," he murmured. "You look like you're ready to jump my bones, and there are children everywhere." With a wink, he got to his feet.

She sighed as he walked away. He was everything she'd ever dreamed of in a man—sexy, funny, intelligent and more empathetic than he knew. He had so much to offer for the long haul. Yet he thought he was only good for a short trip.

He wanted more. He wanted it with an intensity that had caused him to run for cover earlier tonight. He'd been desperate to conceal his emotional reaction and his vulnerability.

Sarah had sensed it, though. And Molly understood it better than he thought she did. She'd discovered tonight how fiercely he clung to his belief about himself. That wouldn't change overnight.

If he could spend a couple of weeks surrounded by this loving family, his rigid stance might shift. Maybe he would come back for visits, and over time, he might realize that living without the joy that he witnessed here was unacceptable. She clung to that hope for his sake.

She, however, would stick to her resolve not to discuss this again. That wouldn't be easy. But unless she wanted him to avoid her completely, she'd have to keep her opinions to herself for the next two days.

Yet she couldn't dismiss his behavior with Sarah Bianca, even if he was ready to. He'd treated the little girl with respect and hadn't tried to put her in her place when she boasted about things she might never do. Molly remembered being that age. Her parents had backed her on all her dreams and schemes.

She wondered if he understood that his kindness and generosity of spirit were unlikely to disappear if he became a husband and a father. No, he probably didn't understand that, and she had to keep herself from pointing it out.

Still, she was convinced that they'd been destined to meet. Whether their meeting was to end up in a brief interlude or something more was a big question mark. So much depended on the next two days.

As Watkins, Trey and Ben prepared for their next set, Mary Lou came down the hallway from the kitchen carrying a three-tiered chocolate birthday cake. It was topped with candles arranged in a circle, although certainly not seventy of them.

The guest sang along as the musicians played "Happy Birthday." Mary Lou set the cake on the bar and Sarah blew out the candles with one breath. A cheer went up. Then plates appeared and Sarah parceled out the cake, starting with the grandchildren.

Molly walked over to where Morgan stood jiggling her youngest, baby Matilda, on her hip. Morgan had tamed her curly red hair with a Celtic-patterned silver clip at her nape, and the fabric of her dress swirled around her in a shimmering cascade of blues and greens. She looked like a Celtic goddess. "Hey, Molly! Having a good time?"

"I'm having a great time. But I have to ask, was that just a random number of candles?"

"Oh, no. Seventy would have made a bonfire, so Sarah asked for a candle for each of us—her three boys and their spouses, her five grandchildren, and Pete. Twelve candles."

"What a great idea."

"I love it. I'm going to steal it for my birthday. I don't need thirty-plus candles on my cake, for God's sake. By the way, I made Gabe email you his genealogy form before he came to the party."

Molly laughed. "Thanks. I know he wasn't overjoyed at having to do it, but I think he'll be glad when he gets the final result. I'll have it bound, with room to add information about the next generation." She smiled at Matilda, who reached up and tried to grab one of her earrings. She dodged out of the way and let the baby catch her outstretched finger, instead.

"That's mind-boggling, you know? People tell me that once SB starts school next fall, time will fly. I can't imagine her in high school, let alone college. And after that, who knows? She could be anything, do anything."

"She told Ben she planned to make a saddle."

Morgan laughed. "I wouldn't put it past her. She was fascinated with that saddle and asked if she could go talk to him about it. I was watching. He seemed to treat her plans very seriously."

"He did. He was so good with her, but—"

"But?"

Molly shook her head. "It's not my place to say. I shouldn't have added that. He was good with her. End of story."

"I doubt it." Morgan's aquamarine eyes filled with understanding. "If you're noticing his behavior with kids, that's a sure sign you're getting invested."

"I am."

"But I'm guessing there are issues."

"Yes."

"There usually are." Morgan plucked a tissue out of a hidden pocket in her dress and dabbed some drool from Matilda's mouth. "But that doesn't mean you can't work them out. It's just too bad you have to leave on Monday."

"Yeah, the timing sucks, but I want to be home for Christmas."

"Of course you do, but you two could keep in touch. You get a spring break, right? Come back up then. Sheridan's not that far. I'll bet he'd drive over to see you."

"Maybe."

Morgan chuckled. "Oh, I'd count on it. I've seen the way he looks at you. And this place has a way of bringing couples together." Her attention shifted back to where the three musicians had been joined by her sister Tyler and Tyler's husband, Alex. "There's a classic example. My little sister was determined to travel the world, but then she met Josie's brother and now she seems perfectly happy in Wyoming working for the Shoshone Chamber of Commerce and doing gigs with Watkins and Trey."

"I really wish I didn't have to leave so soon." Molly

clapped her hand over her mouth. "I can't believe I said that. I've never missed a Christmas with my family. I'd be devastated and so would they."

Morgan's gaze was compassionate. "Well, then, I hope you make it home."

"Me, too." But she was more conflicted than she'd realized. For the first time in her life, she wanted to be in two places at once. And it all had to do with the man who was currently playing a haunting rendition of "Greensleeves" on his harmonica.

Although it was a Christmas song, it was also a love song, and she remembered Ben's promise that every note was for her. He played with an emotional depth that silenced the chatter in the room. Watkins and Trey muted their playing so that Ben's harmonica took center stage.

When the number ended, applause erupted and Molly clapped loudest of all. A man who played a song with that much heart was incapable of becoming a cruel dictator. Maybe someday she would be able tell him that.

After the applause died down, some of the guests took their leave. The crowd gradually thinned out until it included only the core group honored by those twelve candles plus Molly, Ben, Mary Lou and Watkins. Trey had left with his fiancée, Elle Masterson, but Watkins shared Mary Lou's apartment next to the kitchen, so he could continue to provide music without having to worry about the weather.

At last Jack asked for everybody's attention. "It's time we made a decision. If we all leave now, we can probably get home okay. But if we wait much longer, the ranch roads will be impassable."

"You know you can all stay," Sarah said. "Pete and I would love to have you. With Cassidy away on vacation, you'll have to make your own beds, but I know you're all capable of that."

"I wanna stay!" Sarah Bianca said. "I can make my bed!"

"Me, too!" Archie clutched Jack's hand. "Me, too, Daddy!"

"I'd like to stay." Lester stepped forward and put a hand on Archie's shoulder. "I like it when we all sleep over. It's cool."

"Yeah, man." Archie gazed up at Lester with adoration.

Lester blushed. "Sorry. I taught him that."

"You could have taught him a lot worse things, son." Nick glanced around at the group. "I'm for staying and finishing this birthday up right. Who's with me?"

"I am." Dominique stepped up beside him. A tall, elegant brunette, she was a professional photographer who'd been snapping pictures all night. "But when it's bedtime, I get the top bunk."

Nick laughed. "Nice try. We'll draw straws like we always do."

"Somebody can have my bed." Ben said. "I'll camp out in the living room."

"I'll accept your generosity, Ben." Jack looked extremely happy about the turn of events. "Josie and I will take your room. If I know Archie, he'll want to be in with Lester."

Archie grabbed Lester's hand. *"Yeah, man."*

"But you don't have to sleep on the floor, Ben," Sarah said. "Move into Cassidy's room across the hall. She won't mind."

"And our family will take the other bunk room," Morgan said. "See? It works out perfectly!"

"It does, doesn't it?" Jack smiled.

Molly could tell that Jack was glad that they'd all be together on this special night. But he also might be pleased about the bonus. Thanks to the weather, she and Ben had a dozen chaperones staying in the house.

15

NOW THAT NO one had to leave, the party became even more boisterous. Ben wouldn't have thought that was possible, but being snowbound seemed to bring out the goofiness in the Chance brothers. They didn't get drunk, but now that they didn't have to worry about driving, they sure got happy as they allowed themselves to imbibe more freely.

As the music continued, courtesy of Watkins and Ben, Jack organized a dance-off and appointed Molly to judge.

"Oh, no." She waved both hands in denial. "Not doing that, cousin, especially all by myself. I'll get in way too much trouble." Along with the other women, she'd taken off her heels and added them to the pile in the corner.

"I'll help her judge!" Sarah Bianca stepped up next to Molly.

"So will I." Lester joined SB.

Jack surveyed the trio. "Looks like we have us a panel of judges, just like *Dancing with the Stars*. Does that work better for you, Molly?"

Sarah Bianca gazed up at her. "Please?"

"Okay." Molly hugged the little girl. "If you and Lester are going to help me."

"We will." SB nodded solemnly. "Lester and me will be very good judges, right, Lester?"

"Good but tough," Lester said with a grin.

"But *tough*." SB's eyes gleamed. "Very tough."

"All righty! That's settled." Jack clapped his hands together. "And to make it interesting, we'll draw for partners. I'll put all our names in a hat."

Gabe choked on his beer. "*All* our names?"

"Yep." Jack had located a pad of paper and was tearing a sheet into strips.

"So I could end up with you?"

Jack smiled. "Yes, and you'd be lucky to have me."

Ben began to get a sense of just how crazy this family could be. He really was a stranger to this kind of nutty behavior, but as he watched the joking and laughter he realized it could only happen when people were accepted and loved for themselves.

Mary Lou came out of the kitchen to watch as names were drawn. She walked over to Watkins and Ben. "Bet you've never seen this kind of nonsense before, have you, Ben?"

"Can't say as I have." Pete drew first and got Nick as his partner. Ben chuckled as they went into the hallway to practice their moves. "But it's fun."

"I've been the cook at this ranch for thirty-three years, and I thank my lucky stars every day that Archie Chance decided to hire me. I love those boys as if they were my own."

Envy pricked Ben once again. Jack, Nick and Gabe had been blessed with not one, but two mother figures.

Then he remembered Sarah's earlier comment that he was welcome here anytime.

Maybe he couldn't make up for twenty-eight years in a few days, but if he came back often enough, he might begin to feel like part of this family. Sarah seemed to be very good at adopting people. He'd noticed during the party that she'd acted as if Trey was one of her boys. Emmett's son-in-law, Clay, also seemed to be like a son to her. In fact, he could count a bunch of guys he'd put in that category—Josie's brother, Alex. Jack's friend, Nash. And Morgan and Tyler's brother, Regan.

He'd have the perfect excuse to keep coming back if he bought Calamity Sam and got serious about starting a small breeding program. He'd use this family as a role model, and maybe, with continued exposure, he'd gain enough confidence to ask a woman to share his life. Sadly, it might take months or even years, and by then Molly would have found her perfect family man.

That was as it should be. She had no business waiting around for him to get his act together. Besides, it might never happen. He'd had a few beers himself, so he could be building castles in the air.

Pete and Nick took the floor as the first couple in the dancing competition, and Ben quickly forgot his problems. Both of them were determined to lead, and it looked more like a wrestling match than dancing. Watkins had it easier because he could laugh all he wanted to, but Ben struggled to keep a straight face so he could play the harmonica.

"No swearing!" Dominique called out, grinning broadly. "Remember the kids!" Then she raised her camera.

"Don't you dare!" Nick scowled at her and kept trying to steer Pete around the floor. In the process he stepped hard on his partner's toe.

"Sh—ugar!" Pete gritted his teeth and limped through the final bars of the tune.

Meanwhile Molly had been busy making notes as she watched the performance. When the dance was over, she consulted with her panel and they each held up a number. Lester gave them an eight, but SB and Molly each held up a five.

Cheers, groans and raucous comments followed. Josie and Gabe were up next and did much better, getting a seven and two eights. Then Morgan partnered with Dominique, and Ben was impressed with how smoothly they danced. The judges gave them all nines.

That left Jack and Sarah. From the moment they took the floor, Ben knew it was no contest. Obviously mother and son had been dancing together for years, probably at every family event since Jack was a kid.

It was beautiful to watch them dance, but Ben was even more captivated by the expressions of love on the faces surrounding the dance floor. Obviously no one objected to losing to this pair. They'd probably expected it as soon as Jack and Sarah had turned out to be partners. Everyone cheered and hollered when the judging panel gave them three tens.

As the commotion died down, Nick held up his phone. "I just checked the weather, folks. It's not looking so good through the weekend."

Like old-time gunslingers, every man in the room except Ben pulled out his phone. After some muttered comments, Jack was the first to speak. "Good thing we all like each other. We may be here for a while."

THE BLIZZARD RAGED through Sunday night, and Ben had never been through forty-eight hours quite like it. He couldn't so much as kiss Molly. No corner of the house was safe and he was frustrated as hell.

On the other hand, he was given an education in the inner workings of a large, happy family that spanned three generations. Sure, there were disagreements now and then, and sometimes the kids got on everyone's nerves. But inevitably someone would crack a joke to diffuse any tension, or dispense a hug, or suggest a new board game.

Sarah was the linchpin of the operation. She made sure that clothes were washed and a schedule was kept. The littlest ones took their naps as if they were at home, and after the free-for-all buffet of Friday night, the menu shifted to plenty of healthy food and only occasional sweets. Sarah also hauled out colored construction paper to make chains and tissue paper for snowflakes. The adults created some impressive popcorn-and-cranberry garlands.

Fortunately the electricity stayed on all weekend. The ranch hands in the bunkhouse had enough food to last them for a couple of days, and they were close enough to the barn that they could keep the horses fed. Blizzard conditions weren't uncommon and the hands knew what to do.

Ben also noticed that although everyone felt free to joke about most anything, there was never an edge to their teasing. Family members respected each other and were never mean. At first, Ben had wondered if they were putting on a good face for him, and maybe for Molly. But as the weekend continued, he realized that was impossible. Nobody could fake it for that long.

He would have preferred more alone time with Molly, but if he couldn't have that, at least he was getting a crash course in healthy family dynamics. He couldn't tell for sure how Molly was handling the situation because they literally had no private time to talk. She'd mentioned to the entire group that she was worried about getting out on Monday, but other than that, she'd thrown herself into the activities with her typical sunny optimism.

Sometime during the night on Sunday, the snow stopped, and the weak morning sunlight revealed a world covered in generous dollops of whipped cream. Ben hadn't been able to see anything through the frost-covered window in the small room he'd appropriated that normally belonged to Cassidy, the housekeeper, so he'd dressed quickly and headed downstairs to look out the windows protected by the porch roof. He found nearly everyone else down there, too, peering at the snowfall and discussing the options.

Molly was among them, wearing a fleece, moose-print bathrobe on it. The robe made him smile, but it filled him with regret, too. She'd promised to wear it when she headed to his room on Friday, back when another three nights of great sex had seemed possible. Now it seemed unlikely that he'd ever get to watch her take it off.

Jack was there, unshaven and obviously intent on a plan. "According to what I'm finding online, the snowplows are out and the airport is hoping to be operational today. If we can get the road cleared from the house to the highway in time, then Molly can make her flight."

Ben nodded and avoided Molly's gaze. "Sounds good. Do you need help with the plowing?" He didn't want her to go, but this was what she wanted. He'd do what he could to make it happen.

"We'll handle it. You and Molly get yourselves packed, have some breakfast, and be ready to head out."

"I'm outta here." Molly hurried up the curved staircase.

Ben forced himself not to gaze after her like some adoring puppy. Instead, he kept his focus on Jack.

"I'll clear as much as I can," Jack said, "but I may end up plowing in front of you for the last little bit."

"Got it." Ben glanced around at everyone gathered by the window. "What about the rest of you? You must want to get home, too."

"We do," Nick said, "but Molly is the priority. That's the road that needs to be plowed first. We'll worry about the ranch roads once she's on her way."

"Okay."

"Oh, and not to alarm you unnecessarily," Nick added, "but there's another storm headed this way. Molly will probably get out okay, but if the road to Sheridan looks dicey, just come on back here instead of risking the drive."

"Thanks." Ben was touched. "I will. I'll go get my stuff together."

Less than twenty minutes later he sat in the kitchen eating the eggs, bacon and biscuits that Mary Lou had prepared in large quantity. Morgan, Josie and Dominique were there making sure their kids had some breakfast before the start of what promised to be a rigorous day.

Ben glanced at Morgan, who was directly opposite

him with her three kids. "So, you'll all go back home today, I guess."

"We will." Morgan sat with Matilda in her lap while her two-year-old son, Aaron, perched on a booster seat on one side. Sarah Bianca was kneeling in a regular chair on the other side. "I hope you can make it home okay, though. Promise you'll turn around and come right back if there are any issues with the road to Sheridan."

SB gazed at him across the table, her expression grave. "You don't live here?"

"No, I live in Sheridan."

"I've never been there. Do you live with your mommy and daddy?"

"No. I live by myself."

"All by yourself?" She looked dismayed. "Do you even have a Christmas tree?"

He was tempted to lie because he could imagine how the truth would shock her. Finally he compromised. "Not yet."

She cocked her head and stared at him as if digesting that information. "You'd better come back here for Christmas."

"Well, thank you, but I plan to spend Christmas in Sheridan."

"Why?"

A very good question for which he had no answer. "It's where I live."

"But you're all by *yourself.*"

Morgan put a hand on her daughter's shoulder. "SB, some people enjoy that."

Her little face puckered up in thought. "Do you?"

He was saved from answering by Molly's arrival.

Molly was one of SB's favorites, and the little girl quickly abandoned him. Nobody could ask as many awkward questions as a four-year-old. She'd zeroed in on the very subjects that had been troubling him all weekend. After spending nearly four days at the Last Chance Ranch surrounded by happy people, he would be damned lonely in the small apartment attached to his saddle shop.

He took one last gulp of coffee before excusing himself to go fetch his truck while Molly ate her breakfast. The trip to Jackson would be bittersweet. At last he'd be alone with her, but he'd be busy navigating the road and driving her to catch a flight that would take her far away from him.

His truck didn't want to start, but eventually he coaxed the engine to life. After letting it warm up, he backed it out of the shed and drove along the plowed lane Jack had created that led to the circular driveway in front of the house. He left the motor running and the heat blasting as he headed back into the house.

Although he'd promised himself he'd return, and often, leaving created a hollow feeling in his chest. Or maybe it was the thought that he would soon have to say goodbye to Molly. He hadn't allowed himself to think much about that, but the knowledge hovered in the back of his mind, ready to take center stage when he dropped her off at the airport.

Molly's suitcase and carry-on sat by the front door. She'd put on her red coat and she was busy hugging everyone within reach and thanking them for their hospitality. She had a catch in her voice.

But when she noticed Ben standing there, she gave him a bright smile. "Ready?"

"When you are."

She turned back to the little group that had gathered to tell her goodbye. "I'll email, and I'll see about coming during spring break. If that doesn't work out, then I'll definitely be back in the summer."

"Make sure you do that." Sarah gathered her close for one more hug. "But regardless, Pete and I will see you in Arizona."

"Great." She took a shaky breath. "I'd better get out of here before I start bawling." She picked up her carry-on.

Ben took that as his cue. He stepped forward and held out his hand to Sarah. "Thank you for your hospitality. It's been an incredible experience."

She glanced at his outstretched hand, bypassed it and gave him a fierce hug. He hugged her back and was worried for a moment that he might lose his cool. But he cleared the huskiness from his throat and promised to visit soon.

Then he smiled at everyone, grabbed Molly's suitcase and beat it out the door. Their warmth toward him felt great, but he didn't trust himself not to go all sappy and mushy as a result. Molly could get away with it, but he was a guy, and one who'd only just met them all.

He didn't feel that way, though, as he helped Molly into the truck. When he got behind the wheel, he glanced over at the house and saw them all massed in the open doorway, waving. His eyes misted.

Beeping the horn, he pulled out. "They'll freeze their asses off doing that."

"They don't care."

"I know. That's what makes them all so wonderful."

"They are, aren't they?" Molly's voice was a little

shaky as she turned to look at the receding view of the house. "I wish I hadn't taken so long to come up here."

"So you're coming back over your spring break?" He shouldn't ask, but he couldn't seem to help it.

"I might." She faced forward.

Now what was he going to say? That he wanted to see her if she flew up here again? Of course he did, but he was still the wrong guy for her, so he had no business continuing the relationship.

"From your silence I gather you won't be driving over here to see me." Her voice was tight and she stared out the windshield instead of looking at him.

"You know I want to."

"Then why not do it?" She glanced over at him. "What's the harm?"

"Damn it, next you're going to suggest we can be friends."

"You'd be wrong there, cowboy. We can be friends if you want, but mostly I crave your body."

He risked a quick look at her and she had a saucy little smile on her face. He couldn't help laughing. "I see how it is."

"I should hope so. We'd planned on another three nights of hot sex. That didn't happen."

"You noticed." He grinned.

"I certainly did. So if I come back up here on my spring break, do you think you could work those three nights into your busy schedule?"

"Yes." God, but he didn't want her to leave. She was everything he'd ever wanted and more. "I think that can be arranged."

16

MOLLY HAD TWO objectives for this trip to the airport with Ben—to put them both at ease, and to establish that this wasn't a permanent goodbye. She was proud of herself. She'd accomplished both goals in the first two minutes.

Now they could talk easily for the rest of the trip. They caught up with Jack and followed the tractor as it slowly carved a path to the highway. At the end of the road Ben honked the horn in farewell and they were on their way to Jackson.

"Are you definitely coming back for spring break?"

She turned toward him. "Are you definitely driving over from Sheridan if I do?"

"Yes."

"Then I'll be here for spring break."

"Good."

She cherished the enthusiasm in his voice. This wasn't the end, after all. She didn't need promises of forever. It was too soon for that, but at least she'd been given a reprieve from the awful prospect of never seeing him again.

"I'll probably visit the ranch before then, though."

He drove below the speed limit. The road had been plowed, but patches of ice remained. "I'll be making saddles for all three of the guys in exchange for Calamity Sam."

"That's terrific." Thank God she hadn't somehow screwed up his business opportunity at the Last Chance. "They're getting a great deal."

"So am I. Calamity Sam will bring in stud fees that should eventually allow me to buy a mare. Morgan gave me the name of a real estate agent she knows in Sheridan, and as soon as I get home, I'll start looking at horse property. If I can find a place that has a studio I can use for my saddle business, I can give up the shop I'm renting in town."

"I'm excited for you, Ben. Sounds like fun." It also sounded like permanence. He'd already established a business there. Once he bought property and horses, he'd be there to stay.

All weekend she'd watched him interact with the Chance clan and she'd detected a subtle shift in his attitude. He no longer tried to protect himself from the emotional pull of that family. He might think his business deal with the Chance brothers was the link between him and the ranch, but she thought it was more likely an excuse to spend time there.

She predicted that by summer he'd be making regular trips between Sheridan and Jackson Hole, and the visits wouldn't always be about horses and saddles. He was going to let the Chance family adopt him.

Moisture gathered in her eyes, and she quickly blinked it away. They were happy tears, she told herself. This was the best thing that could happen to Ben.

But it meant the end of a dream she'd barely admitted to having. Now that it was dead, she realized how much she'd wanted it. What a foolish fantasy, too. There'd never been a real possibility that he'd someday bond with her immediate family and move to Arizona.

As much as she longed to see him at spring break, maybe it was a dumb move on her part. She should have thought it through before making that suggestion. Early this morning her plan had seemed brilliant, a way to stay connected as, over the next few months, Ben gradually changed his mind about having his own family.

But she hadn't put all the pieces together. The discussions he'd had with the Chance brothers about saddles and horse breeding hadn't included her. Although she'd known he was considering buying property, she hadn't grasped what that meant. By coming back over spring break, she'd only get more hooked on someone who'd put down roots hundreds of miles away.

On the other hand, knowing their parting at the airport wasn't a permanent goodbye would make that moment easier for both of them. But if she was only postponing their inevitable split, was that fair to either of them? Her head began to hurt.

"You're awfully quiet over there."

"Just thinking."

"About what?"

She could admit that she'd been reconsidering whether they should see each other again, after all. But why make the rest of the drive a miserable one for him? "It's not important."

"If it's not important, then you'd tell me, which means it is important and you don't want to tell me."

She liked knowing that he was a smart guy, but in this case, she wished he'd been a little slower on the uptake. Maybe she could talk around the subject. "Leaving you today is going to be hard."

"I know, which is why I'm glad we have the spring break plan. In fact, if you can give me the exact dates, that would make it more real. I can put it on my calendar so I can look forward to it."

So much for that strategy. "I was just thinking that if leaving you today will be tough, then leaving you in the spring will be even tougher."

"Maybe not. You said you could come back in the summer."

She swallowed. She'd done this to herself. If she was willing to come back in the spring and enjoy some good times, then why not repeat it? If she was mostly in it for the sex as she'd implied, then periodic visits to Wyoming made perfect sense.

But although she'd tried to convince herself that great sex was the drawing card, it wasn't anymore. At first it might have been, but she wasn't positive of that, either. She was the optimist who believed everything would turn out all right in the end.

So, naturally, she'd believed a miracle would come along so they could solve their issues. Even his statement about not wanting children hadn't stopped her. Vasectomies could sometimes be reversed, or there was always adoption.

Now he might marry and adopt kids. He seemed to be moving in that direction. But she had a vision of how her life would unfold—her parents as loving grandparents, her brothers and sisters-in-law as cherished aunts and uncles, and their children as cousins and playmates. In Arizona. Within thirty minutes of each other.

"I may be all wet," Ben said, "but I can't shake the feeling that you're reconsidering that spring break plan."

She took a deep breath. "I am, and I'm sorry." She clenched her hands in her lap. "I didn't think it through."

"I wondered about that," he said softly. "It did seem a little too good to be true." He sounded sad, but resigned.

Her heart ached for him. "I *hate* the thought of never seeing you again."

"Likewise."

From the corner of her eye she could see his jaw clench, and she hated that, too. "But I'm…really beginning to care for you."

"I'm not surprised." His voice was tight. "You care for everybody."

"Not the way I care for you."

"Well…" He cleared his throat. "We both know you shouldn't fall for me. So if that means saying goodbye today, that's what we'll do."

She didn't respond to that for fear she'd start crying. And here she'd been so proud of herself because she'd supposedly found a way to make the drive relaxed and fun. It sure wasn't fun now.

After an eternity of silence except for the crunch of the tires on icy patches of road, Ben flipped the turn signal to go into the airport's parking lot.

"You can just drop me off."

"I'm going in with you. I want to make sure you get on the flight okay."

She couldn't very well argue. He was driving. "All right. Thank you."

He insisted on taking charge of both her suitcase and her carry-on, so she was left with only her shoulder bag as they battled a stiff wind on the way into the terminal. The place wasn't very crowded. Several flights had been canceled.

She glanced at the flight information monitor to double-check her flight. Then she blinked and looked again.

"It's canceled," Ben said.

"It wasn't when I checked my phone ten minutes ago!" She heard the desperation in her voice, but she had to get out of here. Part of it was her eagerness to be home for Christmas, but most of it had to do with the man standing by her side. Being with him had become too painful to bear.

Leaving him with the suitcases, she went to the counter, but the woman only confirmed what was on the monitor.

Molly fought panic. "But it's not snowing."

"No, but it will soon. And the winds are treacherous right now. All planes have been grounded until further notice."

Molly groaned. This couldn't be happening.

"I'm sorry." The woman's smile was sympathetic but firm. "We hope to resume service in the morning, so your best bet is to stay close, either in the airport or at one of the hotels nearby."

"Thank you." Taking a deep breath, Molly turned and walked back to where Ben waited with the luggage. "I'll just stay here. Something might open up."

He searched her face, his dark gaze troubled. "How soon?"

She shrugged and did her best to look unconcerned

about it. "Not sure, exactly, but I'll be fine. You'd better take off. Everybody was worried about the road between here and Sheridan, so I don't want you to get stuck."

He blew out a breath and nudged back his Stetson. "Look, Molly, I'm not leaving you here when there's only some vague promise of a flight eventually. Did they say if it would be today?"

"It won't be today, but that's no problem. I can—"

"Damn it, Molly. Did you seriously plan to spend the night here by yourself?"

"Why not?"

He shook his head. "I don't even know where to start. Sure, I know you could do it if you had no other option, but you have another option. Come on." He picked up her suitcase and started toward the door.

"Where are you going?" For one wild moment she wondered if he planned to drive her all the way to Arizona.

"To a hotel."

"Okay." That made more sense. She might have taken a cab to a hotel if he'd left anyway. "You can just drop me at whichever one we come to first."

If he replied she didn't catch it. She was too busy staying upright as they went back to his truck. Maybe the airport authorities knew what they were doing when they'd grounded the planes because of the wind.

He helped her back into the truck and stowed her luggage. She called a couple of nearby hotels to find out which had vacancies. In short order she was able to direct Ben to a medium-priced place that had several rooms available.

As he pulled the truck under the portico at the entrance, she unbuckled her seatbelt and turned to him. "Thank you, Ben. I'm not going to make this a long, drawn-out speech, but I will always cherish what—"

"Good God, woman."

"What?"

"I'm not dropping you off here, either! What do you take me for?"

She gulped. "So, what were your plans?"

"To stay with you until you get a flight out of here, of course, like any decent human being would do. I suppose we could book two separate rooms, but all things considered, that seems like a waste of an opportunity." His gaze was steady.

"Oh." Her heartbeat tripled, at least.

He reached out and brushed a knuckle over her cold cheek. "What do you say, Molly? It seems Fate has thrown us together again. Shall we have one last fling before we call it quits?"

Her chest and throat were so tight it was a wonder she could talk at all. "Okay."

He smiled. "That's my girl."

She thought about those words as they registered and rode the elevator to their third-floor room. *My girl.* It had sounded so sweet, so natural. He'd only meant it as a casual endearment, not a statement of fact, but how she wanted to be his girl. If only the price weren't so damned high.

But she didn't have to think about that, now. Once again, the parameters had been set. They'd enjoy each other for whatever time they had and go their separate ways.

As Ben swiped the keycard, his hand trembled slightly. That was the only outward sign that he wasn't calm and composed about spending the night with her. For her part, after a weekend of wanting and not having, Molly felt like a hand grenade with the pin pulled out.

He stood back and gestured her inside. She walked into an ordinary hotel room with a built-in desk, matching bedspread and drapes, and one easy chair in the corner. There was nothing remarkable about the place.

Then Ben came in and put down her suitcase. When he closed the door and flipped the security latch, she turned to him. In that instant, the room ceased to be ordinary. Her heart pounding, she held his gaze as she unzipped her red parka.

Ben stepped toward her, his dark eyes filled with heat. A shudder moved through his large frame.

She couldn't say who groaned or who moved first, but suddenly they were in each other's arms and tearing at each other's clothes and kicking off their boots. In mere seconds she was down to her underwear, and her glasses were gone…somewhere. She had no idea if she'd taken them off or he had.

And she didn't care, because his talented mouth was covering her with kisses as he stripped off her bra. Her panties ripped as he pulled them down and she didn't care about that, either. When he picked her up, she wound her legs around his waist and pushed her bare breasts against his soft mat of chest hair. Then she bit his shoulder.

His low laugh was the sexiest sound she'd ever heard. "Want this, do you?"

"Desperately."

"That makes two of us." He laid her on the bedspread and followed her down, his rigid cock nudging her damp folds. His first powerful thrust lifted her off the bed.

This time she laughed. "Yes!"

"Yes." The word was almost a growl. Then he began to move, each stroke delving deep into her quivering body.

How she loved the way he claimed her! And there was no other word for it. She surrendered to the delicious sensation of being taken by a man who'd been pushed to the limits of his control.

His heavy breathing blended with her gasps of pleasure as he drove home again and again. His eyes burned with a fierce urgency that sent fire through her veins. She held his gaze as the first tremor rocked her body.

The flame in his eyes leaped and he pumped faster. He coaxed her up, up, until she lost herself in the glory of an orgasm that whirled her like a carnival ride and brought breathless cries to her lips.

He didn't pause, and his command tore through the mists of her climax. *"Again."* He bore down, the rapid friction of his thick cock sending her back to the top of the roller coaster and over into a second screaming descent.

This time he hurtled down with her, bellowing in satisfaction as he pushed deep, his big body shuddering in the grip of his release. Braced on his arms, he gazed down at her as he gulped for air. Gradually his intense expression relaxed into a bemused smile. "You bit me."

She took a shaky breath and smoothed her hand over the red spot on his shoulder. "I know. That's so unlike me."

His glance slid over her and heat smoldered in his eyes. "I don't think so. I think it's exactly like you."

"It isn't! I've never bitten a man in my life!"

"Until me." He sounded pleased with that.

"Unusual circumstances. We had one night of great sex, and one crazy moment in the tractor barn, and then we couldn't do anything because the house was full of people. Naturally I was a little frustrated by that."

His smile was more than a little smug. "I noticed."

"So were you, smarty pants."

"Oh, I won't deny it. This weekend was pure torture. By the time we walked into this room, I was a ticking time bomb. However, I'm not the one who bit." He chuckled. "You are."

"You aren't going to let me forget that, are you?"

"Nope. Because the thing is, under that college professor persona you have going on, you're a wild woman, Molly Gallagher. And until the weather clears, I'm going to prove it to you."

_17_

BEN HAD BEEN given a few more precious hours with Molly, and he planned to make the most of them. When she flew out of here, he would never see her again. He'd known from the beginning he was wrong for her, and now she'd apparently accepted that, too.

But he wouldn't have to face their final goodbye until tomorrow. At this very moment he had a naked Molly lying beneath him, gazing up with those amazing green eyes. He was already getting hard again.

He could stay right where he was and start all over, which would be fine, but he had an unfulfilled fantasy to satisfy. "Let's find your glasses." He eased away from her and climbed out of bed.

"That's very sweet." She sat up. "But if we broke them during that episode, that's okay. I have a spare pair at home and I can wear my contacts in the meantime."

"I hope _I_ didn't break them." He surveyed the carpet as he searched for them. "But thanks for being willing to share the blame."

"They're my glasses, so I should have taken them off if I was worried about them."

A rush of emotion took him by surprise. Pausing in his search, he gazed at her. "Thank you."

"For what?"

"For not blaming me."

Her breath caught. "Oh, Ben." She started to leave the bed.

"Stay there. I can see better than you and you might step on them."

"All right." Her voice was warm with compassion.

The man he used to be would have rejected that compassion. Instead he allowed it to flow over him as it gently soothed a pain he'd never let anyone else see. Dear God, he was going to miss her.

He found her glasses, intact, lying on the carpet. "Got 'em."

"Thanks. Just put them on the nightstand." She smiled and gestured toward his erect cock. "You're blurry, but I can still see that I won't be needing them anytime soon."

"That's where you're wrong." He walked to the side of the bed and handed them to her. "I want you to wear them."

"While we have sex?"

"Yep."

She laughed. "Why, for heaven's sake?"

"Because I love the way you look in them, and it'll be kind of kinky fun to do it while you're wearing glasses and nothing else. But that's not all of it."

She put them on and glanced up at him. "What's the rest?"

"You said you feel more like yourself when you

wear them. I want to make love to you when you're one hundred percent Molly."

She held his gaze. "That's the most romantic thing anyone's ever said to me."

"Really?"

"Yeah."

He soaked up the way she was looking at him, because it made him feel about ten feet tall, and he wanted to remember that warm expression for a long, long time. "Well, good, then." His pulse beating with anticipation, he climbed into bed with her and knelt between her thighs.

"I should warn you they might get in the way of kissing."

"Much as I love kissing you, I have something else in mind." Leaning back, he lifted her legs and propped her heels against his chest.

"My goodness."

"Ever tried it this way?"

"Not while wearing my glasses." Her gaze swept over him and she smiled. "They definitely improve the view."

"For me, too." He took a moment to be thankful for the canceled flight. Otherwise he would never have made love to Molly this way. "I'll take it slow."

"Okay." Her breathing had picked up speed and her skin was the sweetest shade of pink.

His cock throbbed. "Tell me if it doesn't feel good." Cupping her bottom, he lifted her up and watched her reaction as he pushed a little way into her. "All right?"

She groaned softly. "Very right."

Holding her gaze to make sure she didn't flinch, he sank up to the hilt. "Still okay?"

"Yes."

He eased back and rocked forward again. "How about that?"

"Uh-huh."

It was certainly working for him. His fingers flexed as he massaged that firm little bottom of hers while he stroked in and out. Her breasts quivered each time he pushed home and she seemed to grow wetter with each thrust. And those glasses knocked him out. She really was pure Molly with them on, and he was the guy who was about to give her a climax.

She clutched the sheets and gasped. "Ben…I'm… ready to…"

"I know." He felt her first spasm. "Me, too." His climax hovered as if waiting for her. He marveled at how quickly they excited each other, how easy it was to give pleasure and receive it.

He pumped faster. She came, her cries filling the small hotel room. He followed right after. His groans drowned out hers as his climax roared through him.

Shuddering from the impact, he still managed to lower her to the mattress without falling forward and crushing her. Then he eased away from her quivering body without knocking off her glasses. At last, he flopped onto his back and lay there gulping for air. Molly at full power was a force to be reckoned with.

She drew in a shaky breath. "We might have peaked with that one."

Rolling to his side, he propped his head on his hand and gazed at her. "Think so?"

"It was pretty spectacular." She turned her head to look at him. "Or I should say *you* were pretty spectacular. I just went along for the ride."

"You did your part." He brushed his knuckles over her breasts and noticed with satisfaction that her nipples tightened. "Feeling you come is quite a rush for me."

"Feeling you come is amazing." Her gaze was soft and open as if she'd let down all her barriers. "I had no idea making love could feel like that."

She could have said *having sex* and he liked that she hadn't. He liked lying here talking with her about intimate details that only lovers shared. He'd never felt as emotionally connected to someone as he did at this moment.

But the day wasn't even half over yet, and he had more fantasies to fulfill. "Hold still." He gently removed her glasses. "You won't be needing these for a while."

She smiled. "Because we'll be kissing?"

"Showering." Brushing his lips quickly over hers, he left the bed and put her glasses on the nightstand.

"Good plan. You go first since you're already up."

"I have a better idea." He scooped her out of bed and she gave a little shriek. "Ever had shower sex?" He started toward the bathroom.

"That depends on your definition."

He laughed. "Good answer."

"I wouldn't be as likely to have shower sex with a guy wearing a condom, now would I?"

"That's why you're about to have shower sex with a guy who doesn't need one."

"Sounds exciting. I'll bet you're a pro by now."

He lowered her feet to the floor, gathered her close and tilted her chin up so he could look into her eyes.

"I'm not a pro. I've never suggested this to anyone before, but with you I want…everything."

Her eyes widened in obvious shock.

"Hey, I didn't mean it like that." Too late he realized that she might have interpreted that comment as a prelude to a proposal. "I was talking about sex. Don't panic."

"I wasn't panicking. I just wasn't sure what you meant."

"I know. Sorry." Then he kissed her, more to distract them both from a dicey topic than to arouse her. But kissing Molly always got him hot, and soon he had his tongue in her mouth and his hands all over her supple body.

It wasn't until he'd backed her against the bathroom counter and started to lift her up on it that he remembered where they were and why. Shower sex. He set her down with a smile of apology. "Got carried away."

Her eyes were heavy-lidded with desire. "I didn't mind."

"We really are going to get in that shower."

She glanced at his jutting cock. "Better hurry."

"Um, yeah." He had the shower running in no time. He settled the bathmat on the floor and glanced over his shoulder.

She stood there smiling at him.

He held out his hand. "Ready?"

"You know it, cowboy." Sashaying toward him, she put her hand in his.

He helped her into the combination tub and shower and stepped in after her. With her back to him, she stood under the spray and combed her wet hair back from her face. Water cascaded over her curves and made her skin glisten.

A primitive urge that he didn't question took hold of him. Wrapping his arms around her, he drew her close, her back against his heaving chest. Her slippery body drove him wild as he fondled her breasts and slid his hand between her thighs.

She moaned as he thrust his fingers deep. So hot. He made her come in mere seconds, and her cries echoed in the small room. His balls tightened and his cock strained as his body demanded release.

Soon. Easing his fingers free, he turned her to face him. "Wrap your arms around my neck and hold on tight."

She was breathing fast. "Like…in the tractor barn?"

"Exactly like that." Under the shower's liquid caress, he braced his feet apart and lifted her the same way he had in the barn. She wrapped her moisture-slicked legs around his hips as he lowered her onto his waiting cock. He almost came. It felt just that good.

"Ohh." Her low moan told him she completely agreed.

He held still for a couple of seconds while he fought the climax that threatened to overwhelm him. Then he lifted her up and she pushed back down with another throaty moan of delight.

Because they were both so slippery, he didn't dare move too fast, but he didn't have to. The combination of warm water sluicing over them and the gentle slide of his cock was more than enough to send her over the edge, and the minute she clenched around him, he was done for. He came hard with a triumphant cry wrenched from deep in his chest.

Gasping, he held on to her and willed himself to stay steady as he set her gently back on her feet. He didn't let go, because if she was as blindsided by her orgasm as he was by his, she might lose her balance. Or he might. He wasn't absolutely clear on whether he was keeping her from falling or vice versa.

The shower continued to pelt them. When she gazed up at him, her eyelashes were beaded with water. "Shower sex is better than tractor barn sex," she murmured.

He grinned. "Riskier, though."

"No, it's not. You wouldn't let me fall."

Her trust humbled him. "I wouldn't mean to, but—"

"You wouldn't, Ben." Her expression was completely sincere. "Even if I started to go down, you'd block my fall with your body. That's why I was determined *not* to fall. I didn't want you getting hurt trying to protect me."

He bracketed her face with both hands. "And that's the most romantic thing anyone's ever said to me."

She frowned. "You think that's romantic?"

"You just said I'd do anything to keep you safe. No one's…" His stupid emotions were making his throat close up. "No one's ever said that before."

Warmth filled her gaze. "Then I'm glad someone finally did. Now what do you say we get out of the shower before we turn into prunes?"

"Good idea." But he thought about her comment as they dried each other off, as they started fooling around and as they went back to bed to fool around some more. She trusted him. That was huge.

As the day continued, he ordered room service whenever they got hungry because he didn't want to share even one minute of Molly with the outside world. He refused to think about the pain he'd feel the next morning when her plane lifted off.

Except it didn't. The second blizzard arrived before dawn, and when Molly called the airport, she learned that the planes were still grounded. If she was disappointed about that, she didn't show it. Her phone call to her folks in Arizona sounded positive.

Listening to her talk to them, he could tell how much she wanted to get home for Christmas. The snow continued to pile up, though, and he wondered if she'd make it back, after all. But he hid his doubts. Maybe the planes would fly the following morning, December twenty-fourth. Maybe not. She was running out of time.

Now that they'd taken the edge off their sexual hunger, neither of them felt the need to have sex constantly. They watched a movie on TV and then played Candy Crush Saga on her laptop. Whoever scored highest was allowed to choose their next sexual position.

Late in the afternoon, during another game of Candy Crush, played while they sat naked on the bed, she adjusted her glasses and gazed at him. "You're pretty good at being snowbound."

He smiled. "It's easy when I'm snowbound with you." The image of Molly sitting there playing a computer game wearing nothing but her glasses would stay with him a long time.

"Maybe for the first few hours it was, when it was a novelty and we were wild for each other, but you've been stuck with me since yesterday. You've had to use my razor and my deodorant. You've faced the same boring room service choices for every meal. You haven't complained once."

"Neither have you."

"Yeah, like I would. I'm in this fix because I insisted on traveling in December. I have only me to blame, but you've volunteered to keep me company and you've done an admirable job under trying circumstances."

That struck him as funny. He'd been allowed to stay in this cozy hotel room and spend time playing games, watching movies and having amazing sex with Molly Gallagher. The more he thought of her description of that as *trying circumstances,* the broader his grin. Finally he fell back against the pillows, unable to hold back the laughter.

"What's so funny?"

He turned his head to look at her. "You."

"Why?"

"Do you really think this has been a hardship for me?"

"Well, most people would—"

"It's been a privilege, Molly. There's nowhere I'd rather be than right here, keeping you company. The trying circumstances will come later."

Understanding shone in her green eyes and her expression grew tender. She took off her glasses and pushed aside the computer. "We're not there, yet." And she eased her warm body over his and began doing things that made him forget all about what would happen later, when she left Wyoming. And him.

18

BY THE NEXT MORNING, the snow had stopped, and Ben was feeling selfish enough to wish it hadn't. Molly propped herself up against the headboard with pillows, put on her glasses, and called the airport for an update. The news was inconclusive.

She might be able to fly out and she might not, depending on how quickly the snowplows cleared the runways and how dangerous the wind-shear factor was estimated to be. She was advised to come to the terminal and wait it out like everyone else.

"Then that's what we'll do." Ben was willing to spend the day in the terminal if it meant she might eventually be able to fly home.

"But it's Christmas tomorrow. Drop me off there, Ben, and drive back to Sheridan. I insist."

"You can insist all you want, but I'm not going to leave you at the terminal when there's a possibility you'll end up spending Christmas Eve there. And Christmas Day, for that matter."

She pushed her glasses up the bridge of her nose. "Much as I hate to admit it, that could happen."

"It certainly could, and after all this, I won't have you spending Christmas alone in an airport terminal. I can't substitute for your family, but at least you won't be with a bunch of strangers."

She regarded him silently for a minute or two. "Even if I get a flight out, I'll have to make the drive from Phoenix to Prescott, and they've had snow up in the mountains. I'll probably arrive late, after most of the stuff is over. I'll miss the big dinner and the Christmas carols and the kids hanging up their stockings."

The thought of her driving alone into the mountains on Christmas Eve in bad weather chilled his blood, but it wasn't his decision.

"And that's assuming I get a flight out."

He waited for her to sort through this on her own.

"I want to be home for Christmas, but looking at all the facts, I might not make it." She sighed and glanced at him. "If my chances of going home are slim to none, I know what my second choice is. Would you be willing to drive us back to the Last Chance today?"

"Of course, but don't you want to go over to the airport and see if—"

"If we intend to land on the Chance family's doorstep the day of Christmas Eve, they deserve the courtesy of knowing it well in advance. I'll call Sarah and ask if it's okay." She scrolled through her contacts.

"Molly, wait. If we arrive together, and they know I've been with you since Monday, they'll make assumptions. Are you sure that's what you want?"

She lifted her chin. "I'm proud to know you, Ben. They can make assumptions all they want. It won't bother me." Then she hesitated. "Would it bother you? I don't want to come between you and them, either."

"No." He'd already considered whether this would affect his dealings with Jack and had decided that giving Molly a decent Christmas was more important to him. "I'm honored that you've chosen to spend this time with me." He gestured toward her phone. "Make your call."

She did, and of course Sarah told them to come back immediately. In less than an hour they'd checked out of the hotel and were driving back toward the Last Chance. If he'd worried about intruding on Sarah's birthday celebration, that was nothing compared to crashing a Last Chance Christmas. But for Molly he'd risk anything.

Listening to her talk to her folks on the phone was heartbreaking, though. She'd called them as soon as he'd pulled away from the hotel, and the catch in her voice told him how much she'd miss being with them. That was another good reason why she was wrong for him. She'd naturally want to live in Arizona surrounded by her family.

He, on the other hand, had a growing business in Sheridan, and for the first time in his life, a place that felt like home—the Last Chance Ranch. If his business continued to grow, he might rent a storefront in Jackson and hire somebody to run it.

He could even take on an apprentice saddlemaker and teach someone else the skills he'd learned from his mentor. He smiled at the thought that someday Sarah Bianca might go into business with him. Probably not. Kids changed their minds all the time as they grew up, but it was fun to think about.

Molly gazed at the freshly ploughed highway stretching in front of them. Very few vehicles navigated the road. Her pitiful little sigh tore at his heart. "I'm sorry it didn't work out."

"Me, too."

She gave him a quick smile and returned her attention to the road.

When she didn't say anything more, he wondered if she was battling tears. He probably ought to let her work through that by herself.

"My mother said something that surprised me."

"Oh?"

"She thinks this might be a good thing. She doesn't want me to feel tied to the tradition of always being there for Christmas. She pointed out that my brothers have missed a few times."

He proceeded with caution because this sounded like a loaded topic. "What do you think?"

"I don't know. I've always assumed she'd be crushed if I didn't make it home for the holidays. Of course she'll miss me. She said that. But knowing it won't ruin Christmas for her is...liberating, in a way."

"Your mom sounds great."

Molly smiled. "She is great. You would love—well, anyway. Yes, my mom's terrific."

She'd been about to say he'd love her mother. He probably would, but that was beside the point. He would never meet her.

Perversely, now he wanted to. People said you could tell what a woman would be like in twenty-five years by looking at her mother. Despite having no future with Molly, he couldn't help fantasizing about what one would be like.

"I'll bet Jack's out plowing the ranch road so we can

get through." Molly chuckled. "I could be wrong, but I think he likes doing that."

"I can guarantee he does. Most little boys never outgrow their obsession with tractors."

"So I guess you'll be getting one of those, too."

Ben hadn't thought of that. "Guess I will. If I have horse property, I'll need a tractor for raking the corral. And I'll need a blade attachment so I can get in and out in winter."

"You'll also need a name for the place."

"I suppose so. Got any ideas?"

"Oh, tons!" She rummaged in her purse. "This will be fun. Let's make a list."

He smiled at her burst of enthusiasm. God, how he loved…her. *He loved her.* The thought hit him with stunning force. His pulse raced and he lost track of what she was saying. "Hold on to that thought. Let me get past this icy stretch." If he pretended that the road had suddenly become more of a challenge, she might not notice his distracted behavior.

Taking a deep breath, he refocused on the conversation. "Okay, run those past me one more time."

She rattled off several potential ranch names, some decent and some hysterically funny. They debated the merits of those names and came up with more. The subject occupied them for the rest of the drive, but all the while, in the back of his mind, lurked his newfound knowledge. He was in love with Molly Gallagher. And she would never know.

BEN PULLED INTO the circular drive in front of the ranch house behind two vehicles he didn't recognize.

"Oh, I just remembered!" Molly practically bounced

on the seat. "Jack's half brothers, Wyatt and Rafe Locke are supposed to arrive today with their wives. I'll bet that's who's here. Yay! I've been in touch with them for my project, and now we'll meet face-to-face!"

"Then you're okay with not making it home?"

She glanced at him. "I feel like a traitor for saying this, but I'm pretty excited about being here for Christmas now that it's a done deal, especially if I get to meet more family members." She unbuckled her seatbelt and reached for the door handle.

"Molly, hang on a second." He wouldn't bare his soul to her, never that, but he could take advantage of the last few moments of their time alone. "Once we go in there, we won't have any privacy."

She turned to him, her expression contrite. "That's true. Sorry. I didn't mean to rush out of here."

"You're eager to meet them all. I understand."

"But we really will be in a goldfish bowl for the next couple of days. I've considered braving it out and announcing that we'll share a room. I've been debating that ever since we agreed to come back, but I don't think it would be appropriate."

"No, it wouldn't. Before we go in, though, I want to wish you Merry Christmas." He gave her a wry smile. "Minus the gift."

"No apologies necessary. I don't have one for you, either." She touched his face. "But ever since I met you, you've been teaching me what a sexy woman I can be. That's quite a gift, when you think about it. You're precious to me, Ben."

"As you are to me." Nudging his hat back with his thumb, he slid her glasses off and laid them carefully on the dash. Then he cupped her face in both hands. "Merry Christmas, Molly."

"Merry Christmas, Ben."

He took her mouth gently, reverently. It wouldn't be the last time his lips touched hers. He planned to drive her back to the airport after Christmas, but that kiss would be all about goodbye. This one was all about gratitude…and love.

Her response was filled with such unspeakable tenderness that his breath caught. Slowly, reluctantly, he lifted his head and looked into her eyes.

They were filled with wonder, as if she'd just had a revelation.

Hope blazed within him. Maybe, just maybe…

The massive front door flew open and people he didn't recognize poured out chattering and laughing. They clattered down the steps toward the truck with an older woman in the lead, a brunette who had Jack's coloring.

Ben put his money on that being Diana, the runaway wife and mother, which meant the rest of the posse could be her sons and their wives. "Your welcoming party is here."

Molly put on her glasses just as the woman leading the pack rapped on her window. With a start of surprise, Molly looked out. Then she opened the door, letting in a cold blast of air. "Hi."

"Hi! I'm Diana, and these are your long-lost cousins, or step-cousins, or whatever the terminology is, Wyatt and Rafe. Oh, and their dearly beloveds, Olivia and Meg. Come on in! After all those emails, we're dying to meet you!"

Molly turned back to Ben. "Listen, I hate to—"

"Go ahead." He gave her a smile. "I'll bring the luggage."

Belatedly Diana glanced at Ben and seemed to remember her manners. "Sorry, how rude of me! And now I've forgotten your name."

"Ben."

"Kids, this is Ben, the guy who made that amazing saddle."

A chorus of greetings and compliments went up from the group. Then Molly climbed out, and their attention shifted to her. That gave Ben the leisure to study everybody.

One of the guys was the spitting image of Jack, only a few years younger, so he had to be Rafe, who managed investment portfolios. Ben should probably talk to him before the holiday was over, considering all his plans for expansion.

The sandy-haired stepbrother must be Wyatt, who owned an adventure trekking operation. Ben observed body language to figure out the pairings, and he found the matchups fascinating. The pulled-together woman, Olivia, was with Wyatt, while Meg, the wholesome one with the freckles, was Rafe's bride.

He waited until they'd all gone inside before unloading the luggage. After setting his duffle bag and Molly's suitcase on the porch steps, he drove his truck down to the barn and parked. Much scraping and shoveling must have gone on this morning, because the entire area was clear of snow. Huge mounds of the stuff had been dumped to the side of the buildings, though. Sled tracks and snowball forts told him that the kids had enjoyed themselves today.

As he walked back to the house, he thought about

the look in Molly's eyes after their kiss. If he didn't know better, he'd swear she'd just figured out that she loved him. If so, then what?

He was still a serious gamble for her. She obviously thought he had no reason to be concerned about his potential as a husband and father. But he was afraid that some little thing could flip a switch, and he'd become his dad.

He stepped through the front door into a world of joyful chaos. Christmas carols were on the sound system and Sarah's grandchildren raced through the living room in delirious glee. Christmas Eve was only hours away. Anticipation hummed in the evergreen-scented air.

His saddle—no, *Sarah's* saddle, was still in its place of honor beside the Christmas tree. Leaving the suitcases in the entryway for now, he meandered over to take another look at the project that had brought him to this place. To Molly.

Damn, but he was proud of it. He ran his hand over the seat and remembered how he'd struggled to fit the leather just right. The stirrups hung straight and true, and the tooling was…wait a minute. He crouched down and peered at the intricate work.

Dear God. Somebody, some *kid*, had scribbled on the leather with a neon green felt pen. His work, his labor of months, had been defiled, and recently. He could smell the acrid scent of fresh marker. Gut churning, he stood and scanned the room.

Archie, Jack's tow-headed three-year-old, met his gaze. He held a neon green pen in his chubby fist.

Anger seethed as Ben glared at the child. *"Archie."*

Archie stared back, his gaze stricken. "I made it… pretty."

All conversation in the room stopped. Jack put down his beer and looked from Ben to his son. "Archie, what did you do?"

"I…I colored it." His lower lip quivered.

Jack's expression was thunderous. *"You marked on Grandma's saddle?"*

"I wanted to make it nice, Daddy!" the little boy wailed.

Jack started toward him, fire in his eyes. "That is not acceptable, young man! You are in big—"

"Jack." In that moment, Ben remembered being that age and screwing up. Archie was so small. So vulnerable. Instinctively Ben knew that Jack wouldn't harm the kid, but anger was not appropriate here. Understanding was. Ben moved between father and son. "It's okay. It can be fixed."

"Archie needs to understand that he can't do this kind of thing."

Ben looked down at the little boy. "I think you already know that, don't you, sport?"

Archie nodded vigorously.

"So, tell you what. You and I will get some alcohol and we'll clean this off, okay?"

Archie nodded again, his eyes wide.

Sarah approached. "I'll help." She crouched down next to her grandson. "I know you were only trying to decorate it."

His voice was a faint whisper. "I was, Grandma."

Sarah glanced up at Ben. "Thank you for understanding. He's learning."

"Yeah, I know." Ben's throat felt tight. And he knew

something else. He'd been tested just now, and he'd passed with flying colors. He was *not* like his father.

Someone touched his arm and he turned to see Molly standing there, that same look of wonder in her eyes.

"Could I—" She cleared her throat. "Could I talk to you for a moment?"

"Sure."

Taking his hand, she led him out of the room and down the hallway into the large dining room, which was empty. Light spilled in from the busy kitchen, but the room was still mostly in shadow.

Molly took his other hand and faced him. "I love you."

His world tilted.

"You put your heart and soul into that saddle, and Archie messed with it. If you were ever going to become a bully like your father, you would have done it then."

"I know." And suddenly it was all so easy. "I'll move to Arizona. I'm sure there are people there who need custom saddles. As for Calamity Sam, I'll—"

"You'll buy him and stay right here in Wyoming."

"No." He shook his head. "I can't ask you to leave your family."

"You're not asking me to. I'm offering. My folks have a great ranch that they'll pass on to my brothers. Sure, they'd give me a share, but when you and I started tossing around names for your ranch, I realized that I want to be part of something that I've helped build, something that hasn't existed before. I want us to be like Archie and Nelsie, creating a life from the ground up."

Joy threatened to turn his brain to mush, but he

forced himself to ask the necessary questions. "What about your job?"

She shrugged. "You have a college in Sheridan. I'll apply to teach there, or get licensed for public school. I don't see that as a problem." She hesitated. "But I've done most of the talking. Maybe I'm jumping to conclusions. Maybe you don't—"

"Of course I love you." His heart thudded wildly. "I'm crazy about you."

Even in the darkness, her smile was dazzling.

"Excellent." She lifted her mouth to his. "You and I are going to make history."

As he kissed her, he had no doubt of that. Molly Gallagher, source of all things wonderful, would see to it.

Epilogue

CADE GALLAGHER HAD called home every Christmas Eve since he'd left Thunder Mountain Ranch, but he felt an unexplained urgency this year. Maybe it had to do with being several hundred miles away in Colorado and sitting in an empty bunkhouse. All the other hands had gone into town, but he'd chosen to stay here and make this special call. He missed Rosie and Herb Padgett, the people he'd come to call Mom and Dad.

He also missed Lexi, but that was nothing new. Missing her was a constant nagging ache that hadn't gone away even after five years. She was the reason he hadn't felt comfortable going back to Sheridan in all this time. Because her parents were good friends with the Padgetts, she'd spent plenty of time at Thunder Mountain Ranch. Still did, judging from stray remarks during phone conversations with Rosie.

He called the ranch's land line. Cade liked picturing Rosie answering in the kitchen while stirring her famous vegetable stew—a Christmas Eve tradition at Thunder Mountain. When all the boys had lived there, she'd made a huge vat of it. Now that it was just her and Herb, she probably made a smaller batch.

"Cade!" She always sounded as if his call was the best thing that had happened to her all day. "I just talked to Finn a minute ago!"

"Yeah? How's he doing?" Cade didn't know how many of the boys called home this time of year, but he, Finn and Damon were faithful about it. They'd been the first three to come to the ranch and their loyalty ran deep.

Homeless preteens within months of each other in age, they'd been desperate to establish an identity. They'd heard about a Native American blood-brother ceremony and had enacted it with typical adolescent drama. They'd named themselves the Thunder Mountain Brotherhood. They still kept in touch, but not as much as they should. Cade often got his news about Finn and Damon from Rosie.

"His microbrewery is keeping him busy, that's for sure. Seattle is a great town for it, apparently. But his divorce became final last month."

"Sorry to hear that. I'll give him a call. How about Damon? Have you heard from him yet?"

"Not yet, but I'm sure I will. He never misses. But you know him, probably out on the town with some woman he met last week. None of them last long, though."

"Nope." Unlike Cade and Finn, Damon had never fallen hard for anyone. Cade didn't ask about Lexi. That would make Rosie think he was still interested. He was, but it was complicated. "So, you and Dad are doing okay?"

"Couldn't be better. Retirement suits us both. Listen,

before I forget, someone called a few days ago. She's working on her family's genealogy chart and asked if I knew a Cade Marlowe. Of course I said I didn't."

A shiver ran down his spine. "If she's from the Marlowe side, I want nothing to do with her."

"Her name is Molly Gallagher, so she could be related to your mother, but don't worry. I didn't give her any information. She thinks she hit a dead end."

"Just as well. I have all the family I need."

"And I love you, too." There was a definite smile in her voice. "But I took her number in case you decide to call and find out if you're related in some way. For what it's worth, she seemed like a nice person."

"I'll think about it." He searched the empty bunkhouse for a piece of scratch paper and finally pulled an envelope out of the trash. "What's her number?" As Rosie read it off, he scribbled it down.

He had no intention of calling now. He doubted that he'd ever call. If his mother hadn't seen fit to contact her family, then why should he? But maybe he'd change his mind in the future, so he tucked the envelope in the cubby where he kept his stuff.

"Lexi's doing fine." Rosie tossed it out exactly as someone might throw a bread chunk to a bird.

He approached cautiously and took a nibble. "Good. What's she up to these days?"

"Teaches riding. She's talented in that area. She was dating some guy but they broke up."

And damned if that didn't make his Christmas Eve a little bit brighter.

"Should I tell her you said hello?"

"Better not."

Rosie sighed. "Cade, I wish you'd come home, just

for a weekend, and talk to her. I can't help thinking that both of you are pining away and are too bull-headed to admit it."

"I'll think about that, too. Merry Christmas, Mom."

"Merry Christmas, Cade. I love you."

"Love you, too. Give my love to Dad." He sat on his bunk long after he'd hung up. He wondered what Lexi was doing.

At least he didn't have to worry about her being with somebody else tonight. When Lexi broke up with somebody, she took her time about dating again. From what he'd heard, she'd waited a year after their split.

He'd waited a hell of a lot longer than that. Finally he'd eased back into the game, but he hadn't found anyone like Lexi. He had a bad feeling he never would.

* * * * *

COMING NEXT MONTH FROM

Blaze

Available December 16, 2014

#827 SEDUCING THE MARINE
Uniformly Hot!
by Kate Hoffmann

Marine Will McIntyre wants two things—to get back to his unit after an injury, and Dr. Olivia Eklund. Olivia is very tempted, but she knows the sooner Will heals, the sooner he'll leave her...

#828 WOUND UP
Pleasure Before Business
by Kelli Ireland

After one mind-blowing night with Grace Cooper, Justin Maxwell demands more from his former student. But Grace has big plans for her future, and every moment with Justin puts that future at risk...

#829 HOT AND BOTHERED
by Serena Bell

Cleaning up an infamous guitarist's reputation shouldn't be that hard for image consultant Haven Hoyt. But once she gets her hands on Mark Webster, neither can resist their attraction—or the temptation never to let go!

#830 AFTER MIDNIGHT
Holiday Heat
by Katherine Garbera

It's New Year's Eve and überserious skier Lindsey Collins resolves to have a sexy fling. But bad-boy snowboarder Carter Shaw is determined to show her he's more than a good time.

REQUEST YOUR FREE BOOKS!
2 FREE NOVELS PLUS 2 FREE GIFTS!

red-hot reads!

YES! Please send me 2 FREE Harlequin® Blaze™ novels and my 2 FREE gifts (gifts are worth about \$10). After receiving them, if I don't wish to receive any more books, I can return the shipping statement marked "cancel." If I don't cancel, I will receive 4 brand-new novels every month and be billed just \$4.74 per book in the U.S. or \$4.96 per book in Canada. That's a savings of at least 14% off the cover price. It's quite a bargain. Shipping and handling is just 50¢ per book in the U.S. and 75¢ per book in Canada.* I understand that accepting the 2 free books and gifts places me under no obligation to buy anything. I can always return a shipment and cancel at any time. Even if I never buy another book, the two free books and gifts are mine to keep forever.

150/350 HDN F4WC

Name _____ (PLEASE PRINT) _____

Address _____ Apt. # _____

City _____ State/Prov. _____ Zip/Postal Code _____

Signature (if under 18, a parent or guardian must sign) _____

Mail to the **Harlequin® Reader Service:**
IN U.S.A.: P.O. Box 1867, Buffalo, NY 14240-1867
IN CANADA: P.O. Box 609, Fort Erie, Ontario L2A 5X3

Want to try two free books from another line?
Call 1-800-873-8635 or visit www.ReaderService.com.

* Terms and prices subject to change without notice. Prices do not include applicable taxes. Sales tax applicable in N.Y. Canadian residents will be charged applicable taxes. Offer not valid in Quebec. This offer is limited to one order per household. Not valid for current subscribers to Harlequin Blaze books. All orders subject to credit approval. Credit or debit balances in a customer's account(s) may be offset by any other outstanding balance owed by or to the customer. Please allow 4 to 6 weeks for delivery. Offer available while quantities last.

Your Privacy—The Harlequin® Reader Service is committed to protecting your privacy. Our Privacy Policy is available online at www.ReaderService.com or upon request from the Harlequin Reader Service.

We make a portion of our mailing list available to reputable third parties that offer products we believe may interest you. If you prefer that we not exchange your name with third parties, or if you wish to clarify or modify your communication preferences, please visit us at www.ReaderService.com/consumerschoice or write to us at Harlequin Reader Service Preference Service, P.O. Box 9062, Buffalo, NY 14269. Include your complete name and address.

HB13R2